THE
BLIZZARD
DISASTER

PEG KEHRET

A MINSTREL® BOOK

Published by POCKET BOOKS
New York   London   Toronto   Sydney   Tokyo   Singapore

A Minstrel Book published by
POCKET BOOKS, a division of Simon & Schuster Inc.
1230 Avenue of the Americas, New York, NY 10020

Text copyright © 1998 by Peg Kehret

Originally published in hardcover in 1998 by Minstrel Books

All rights reserved, including the right to reproduce
this book or portions thereof in any form whatsoever.
For information address Pocket Books, 1230 Avenue
of the Americas, New York, NY 10020

ISBN: 0-671-00962-1

First Minstrel Books paperback printing January 1999

10 9 8 7 6 5 4 3 2 1

A MINSTREL BOOK and colophon are registered trademarks of
Simon & Schuster Inc.

Front cover illustration by Bill Schmidt

Printed in the U.S.A.

For my huckleberry friend

CHAPTER

1

Janis Huff wanted to stay home. She stayed in bed as long as she could, putting off the moment when she would have to go to school.

Usually on Monday mornings, Janis was glad to leave home chores behind and walk the two-plus miles to the one-room country schoolhouse. She liked learning about current events, such as last week's election, when Franklin Delano Roosevelt won a third term as President of the United States. She enjoyed reading, and arithmetic, and practicing her penmanship. She even liked being Miss Colby's assistant and helping the younger children learn their letters.

Peg Kehret

This Monday, Janis did not want to go to school.

Saturday had been the most terrible day of Janis's life, and she feared that today would be even worse. She did not want to go to school because she was afraid of what she would find when she returned home.

Saturday had begun in an ordinary way, with her four-year-old sister, Ellie, tugging on Janis's hand and saying, in a loud whisper, "Are you awake?"

When Janis didn't respond, Ellie tugged harder and spoke louder. "JANIS, ARE YOU AWAKE?"

"Of course I'm awake," Janis grumbled. "How could I not be awake, with you shouting in my ear?"

"Daddy's already left," Ellie said. "He did the chores early and went duck hunting."

It was barely light. Janis pulled her hand away and turned over with her back to Ellie.

"I want you to get up and help me teach Wonderful to shake hands," Ellie said.

"No," Janis said. Ellie often wanted Janis to play with Wonderful, Ellie's imaginary squirrel. Sometimes, to amuse Ellie, Janis went along with the pretense—but not at dawn on a Saturday.

2

The Blizzard Disaster

Ellie chattered on. "Daddy will be back before afternoon chores because Doc Swenson is coming to see Pansy."

Janis opened her eyes and rolled onto her back. "How do you know that?" she said.

"I heard Mommy and Daddy talking. I was under the table looking for Wonderful and they came in the kitchen and Daddy said he talked to Doc Swenson yesterday and Doc is coming to look at Pansy. Daddy thinks Pansy is blind."

Dread crept under the patchwork quilt with Janis. She, too, suspected that Pansy was blind, but she had not told anyone because she was afraid that Daddy would not let her keep a blind horse. If Pansy was sold, Janis did not think she could bear it.

"Is that all?" Janis said. "Did you hear anything else?"

"Daddy might keep Pansy in the cellar."

"What?"

"That's what he said. If Pansy is blind, she has to stay in the cellar."

"That's ridiculous," Janis said. "How would a horse get down those narrow stairs? And there's no room in the cellar, anyway. This time of year it's full of Mother's canning."

3

Peg Kehret

She thought of the dark area beneath the kitchen where the canning jars filled with green beans, corn, peas, tomatoes, applesauce, cucumber pickles, and wild raspberries were stored for the coming winter. In spite of her worry, she smiled as she imagined big old Pansy clomping about, swishing her tail across the glass jars and knocking them from the shelves to the dirt floor.

"Daddy said so," Ellie insisted.

"Exactly what did Daddy say? Think hard and tell me what his words were."

Ellie frowned, concentrating on the remembered conversation. "He said, 'If the horse is blind, I'll have to put her down.'"

"No," Janis said. "Oh, please, God, no. Not Pansy." She flung the quilt back and jumped out of bed.

"What's the matter?" asked Ellie. "What are you going to do?"

Janis dressed quickly and ran downstairs.

"Wait for me," Ellie said as she hunted under the bed for her shoes.

Janis grabbed her sweater from the hook, slipped out the door, and ran across the barnyard. Chickens clucked and squawked, fluttering out of her way.

She lifted the latch on the barn door and

4

stepped inside. Janis loved the smells of the barn: the sweet fresh hay, the horses, the leather halters. She passed Jupiter, the black horse, and stopped at Pansy's stall.

"Good morning, Pansy." The dappled gray mare turned her head toward Janis's voice.

Janis put one hand on each side of Pansy's face and gazed into the old horse's eyes. They looked cloudy, as if a thin white veil had dropped over the pupils.

Pansy's eyes used to be brown—a deep velvety brown—and so expressive that Janis knew what the horse was thinking just by looking at her eyes.

When Janis was born, in 1928, Pansy was already a working farm horse. Together with Jupiter, Pansy pulled the plow and the hay rake, and the clunky wooden manure spreader.

The Huffs had a truck now, but in the early years before the truck, and before Ellie, Pansy also pulled the wagon that carried Mr. and Mrs. Huff and Janis to town to get supplies. Janis remembered sitting on Daddy's lap and being allowed to hold the reins for a time on the way home.

When Janis was six, she had decided to ride Pansy. One day she climbed the fence around the field where Pansy was grazing. When the curious horse came over to see what she was doing, Janis climbed on the broad back, clinging to Pansy's mane.

Unfortunately, getting off was not as simple as getting on. Pansy walked around and around the field, with Janis straddling her back, but she never again approached the fence.

Janis was afraid to let go and slide all the way to the ground, so she rode the mare for hours, until Daddy came looking for her and helped her down.

After that, Janis was allowed to ride Pansy whenever Pansy wasn't being used to do farm work. But she had to let Daddy help her mount and dismount. He said it was too dangerous for her to climb on and off by herself, even with a mellow old mare like Pansy.

From that first ride, Janis had loved Pansy with all her heart and often asked Daddy if he would give Pansy to her. She brushed the mare's thick coat until it shone. Soon the horse whinnied a greeting whenever Janis approached.

In the fall, when apples fell from the trees, Janis carried one every day to Pansy, for a special treat.

The Blizzard Disaster

At Christmastime that year six-year-old Janis had poured over the toy pages in the catalog, wondering aloud what Santa might bring her.

Mother said, "Times are hard, Janis. Even Santa may not be able to afford toys this year."

"Santa doesn't have to pay for toys," Janis declared. "His elves make them."

On Christmas morning Janis had rushed downstairs to the Christmas tree. She found a cornhusk doll and a note.

Dear Janis: Pansy is your horse now. Take good care of her. Love, Santa

Nothing really changed, because Janis was already taking good care of Pansy. Even so, Janis was thrilled. And in the six years since then, she continued to love and care for her horse. Riding Pansy was the perfect way to get off by herself, away from Ellie's constant chatter and Mother's unending chores.

In the last year Pansy had moved more slowly. She refused to pull the manure spreader unless Jupiter was hitched up with her. And once, when Janis was riding her, Pansy had almost walked right into a willow tree.

Peg Kehret

That's when Janis first suspected what Pansy's problem was. But she had said nothing.

Money was tight on the farm. It always had been, ever since Janis could remember. She had never, not once in her twelve years, worn a store-bought dress. Her winter coat was cut from an old blanket, and her Sunday shoes were hand-me-downs from one of her cousins. Janis knew there was no extra money for veterinary care for Pansy.

She had hoped nobody else would notice Pansy's failing eyesight.

Daddy had noticed.

CHAPTER

2

Janis had stayed in the stall with Pansy on Saturday morning until Mother called her to come and gather twigs for kindling. "Your father will cut the firewood for winter this week," Mrs. Huff said, "and we'll need you to stack it. You can do that after school each day, instead of helping me in the kitchen."

Mrs. Huff opened the cookstove and removed a pan of biscuits. "It's late in the year to be getting the firewood ready."

"It's still warm," Janis said.

"It won't stay warm. Not in November. You and Ellie can get the twigs picked up today. Be sure to get the ones under the chestnut tree."

Ellie wasn't much help, but Janis worked quickly, breaking all the small fallen branches into foot-long lengths. She filled a bushel basket with twigs and placed it on the ground outside the kitchen door. A second basket of twigs went in the barn.

She gathered twigs until the noon meal. As soon as she ate, she returned to Pansy and stayed there until she heard the truck drive into the yard. She watched Daddy get out and carry ducks into the house for Mother to pluck.

Janis climbed the ladder to the hayloft and lay near the opening where they tossed hay down to Pansy and Jupiter. She waited.

When Doc Swenson drove up, Mr. Huff came out of the house to greet him.

"I hope you'll accept four fresh ducks as payment today," Mr. Huff said. "Shot them myself this morning, up by Vergas."

"Heard the hunting's been good," Doc said.

"They flew in thick as fleas," Mr. Huff said. "I never saw such a duck run. Makes me think winter isn't far off."

"I didn't have time to go hunting," Doc said, "so your ducks will be welcome."

The two men walked into the barn, and Mr. Huff opened Pansy's stall.

Janis leaned close to the opening, trying to peek over the edge without being seen.

Doc shined a light into Pansy's eyes. He looked carefully at first one eye, and then the other. "It's a shame when this happens," he said. "It's glaucoma, same as people get. My own dear mother lost her sight this way. There's nothing to be done for it."

"She's completely blind then?" Mr. Huff said.

"I'm afraid so."

Above them, Janis closed her own eyes and tried not to cry.

"I'll have to put her down," Mr. Huff said. "I can't afford to keep a horse that isn't able to work."

"There's a lethal injection I can give her," Doc Swenson said. "It's a painless death. But I'd have to charge you for the medication since I have to pay for it myself."

"How much?" Mr. Huff asked.

Janis clapped her hands over her ears. She didn't want to know how much money it would cost to end Pansy's life. When she listened again, she heard Daddy say, "I'll have to do it myself, Doc, with the shotgun. But I'm grateful for your offer."

Janis waited until Daddy and Doc had left

the barn. Then she climbed down the ladder and looked out the barn door. She watched Daddy fetch the four ducks from the house and hand them to Doc. She watched Doc's car drive away.

As soon as Daddy went back into the house, Janis put the halter on Pansy and led her out of the stall and across the barnyard to the orchard. There were still a few rotting apples on the ground, and Pansy nibbled them hungrily.

I won't let him do it, Janis thought. I'll stand in front of Pansy, so he can't pull the trigger.

She waited, watching the house. Her stomach felt as tangled as Ellie's hair when it was freshly shampooed.

"Janis!" She heard her mother call, but Janis did not respond. They want me in the house, she thought, so I won't know what Daddy is going to do until it's done.

"Jan-is!"

She saw Daddy step out on the porch, holding his shotgun. She saw Mother say something to him before he walked away.

"Janis!" Mother's call was shrill now, frantic.

Daddy strode toward the barn, went inside,

and, a few seconds later, came out again. He stood in the farmyard, looking in all directions. When he spotted Janis and Pansy under the apple tree, he walked toward them.

"So you know," he said as he stopped beside Janis.

"You can't do it, Daddy," Janis said. "Pansy is *my* horse. You said so yourself. You can't shoot her."

"I'm sorry, Janis," Daddy said. "I'm fond of old Pansy, too, but a blind horse can't be of any use on a farm. Go inside now. Your mother's calling you."

"No." It was the first time in her life that Janis had ever deliberately disobeyed her father.

"This is hard for me, too," Daddy said. "Don't make it worse than it already is."

"No."

"Pansy's had a good life," Mr. Huff said, "but now she's old and blind. She loved to work, and she can't do it any more. Sometimes death is a kindness."

"Pansy isn't suffering," Janis said. "She can't see, but she's able to walk and eat and she follows Jupiter around. When I ride her, she finds her way home by herself. I think she can tell where she is by the smell." Janis talked faster, trying to fill the air with her own words so that her father could not speak the words she dreaded. "I'll take care of her, Daddy. I'll toss down the hay and carry water and muck out the stall. I'll do everything."

"A horse eats too much to be a pet," Mr. Huff said. "My mind is made up, Janis. Now go inside with your mother and Ellie."

Tears streamed down Janis's cheeks. "If you kill Pansy, Daddy," she said, "I will never forgive you."

Mr. Huff cringed at the word *kill*. "That's enough," he said. "Move away from the horse."

Janis stood with her back to Pansy and spread her arms wide, shielding the mare. Pansy whinnied, a soft low whinny, and stopped eating the apples long enough to rub her face against Janis's outstretched hand.

Janis stared at her father, holding her breath.

Mr. Huff stared back, his jaw clenched. The vein in his temple throbbed.

"Ellie!" Mrs. Huff screamed the word. "Come back here!"

Janis and Mr. Huff looked toward the house. Ellie was running toward them, her hair streaming out behind her.

Janis let out her breath. She didn't think Daddy would shoot Pansy in front of Ellie.

Ellie puffed up to her sister and her father and said, "Are you going hunting again, Daddy? Are you going to shoot some more ducks?"

"Ellie will never forgive you, either," Janis said. "Even if she doesn't see it happen, I'll tell her."

"See what?" Ellie said. "What are you going to tell me?"

Janis waited.

"Nothing," Mr. Huff said. "There's nothing to tell."

"Are you going to ride Pansy?" Ellie asked.

"Yes," Janis said. She grabbed the halter and led Pansy away from the apple tree, toward her father. "Daddy's going to help me mount, aren't you, Daddy?"

"Why are you crying?" Ellie said. "Your nose is all red."

Mr. Huff laid the gun on the ground and gave Janis a boost onto the mare's back. "This is not the end of the matter," he said. "I'll think on it for a day or two."

Janis, unable to speak, dug her heels into Pansy's sides and rode away.

"I want to ride Pansy, too," Ellie wailed. "Janis always gets to ride and I never do."

Mr. Huff picked up the shotgun and headed for the house.

Ellie hurried after him. "When I'm twelve years old," she said, "Pansy will be *my* horse and I won't let anyone else ride her." She thought for a moment and then added, "Except maybe Wonderful."

Janis rode Pansy for an hour and spent the rest of Saturday afternoon either watching Pansy in the orchard or sitting near her in the barn.

Except for church and chores on Sunday, she stayed with the mare that day, too. She wanted to spend as much time as she could with Pansy, and she wanted to be sure Daddy didn't sneak out to the barn with his gun when Janis wasn't watching.

When Ellie hung around, asking questions about why Janis wanted to sit in a boring old barn, Janis refused to answer. Eventually Ellie grew weary of talking to herself and left.

Now the weekend was over, and Janis had no choice but to get out of bed and prepare for school. Filled with anxiety, she dressed and went downstairs for breakfast.

CHAPTER

3

"**W**onderful! Here, Wonderful!" Ellie crawled on her hands and knees into the kitchen, calling loudly. She looked in the box of apples that sat beside the door. She looked behind the woodbox next to the large black cookstove. "Wonderful! Where are you?"

"Ellie, hush," her mother said. "And don't get too close to the stove. You'll burn yourself."

"I can't find Wonderful. He's lost," Ellie said. She crawled to where her sister sat. "Janis, will you help me look for Wonderful?"

Janis ate the last spoonful of her oatmeal and carried her bowl to the sink. "I can't," she said. "I have to go to school." I wish I could stay home today, she thought, but not because of Wonderful.

Mrs. Huff finished ironing a shirt, hung it over the back of a kitchen chair, and reached into her laundry basket for another one. "How can you lose an imaginary squirrel?" she asked.

"Wonderful isn't imaginary," Ellie said. "He's real." Her lower lip trembled.

"Wonderful is probably just playing hide-and-seek," Janis said as she washed her dishes. "Or maybe he doesn't want breakfast today."

"Last night," Ellie said, "Wonderful got out of bed and came downstairs and ate some ginger cookies."

"Oh, Ellie," said Mrs. Huff. "You didn't!" She set the iron on the ironing board and looked in the pottery crock where she kept cookies. "This jar was full yesterday," she said, "and now it's half empty."

"Bad squirrel," said Ellie. "That's why he's hiding."

"You'll be sick if you stuff yourself with sweets that way," Mrs. Huff said. "And don't go blaming a squirrel who doesn't exist."

"I want Janis to stay home from school

today," Ellie said. "I want her to help me find Wonderful."

"Janis has to go to school," Mrs. Huff said.

"Then I want to go to school, too," Ellie said.

"You'll start school in two years," Mrs. Huff said, "when you're six years old."

"And I'll walk to school and back with Janis every day," Ellie said.

"When you're twelve, I'll be done with school," Janis said as she put her dishes in the cupboard. "I'll have a job and live in town, maybe in Minneapolis, in an apartment, and I'll ride the streetcar to work."

"You always get to be the oldest," Ellie wailed. "I want a turn to be the oldest. I want to ride the streetcar."

"That's enough, Ellie," Mrs. Huff said. "Sit down and eat your oatmeal."

"I'm not hungry," Ellie said.

"I can't imagine why not," said Janis as she sliced some bread for her lunch. "Miss Colby shouldn't have school today. Armistice Day is supposed to be a holiday."

"What's Armistice Day?" Ellie asked.

"It's the anniversary of the end of the great war," Mrs. Huff said. "The armistice agreement was signed on November 11, 1918. I was ten years old, and I remember how excited everyone was." She paused, with the iron in midair. "It seems only yesterday," she said, "and here it is 1940 already. I just hope we stay out of the war in Europe. I don't trust that man, Hitler."

"Where's Europe?" Ellie said. "Is Europe by Minneapolis?"

Janis carried her lunch box toward the door.

"Wear a coat, Janis," said Mrs. Huff as she started ironing again.

"It isn't cold out, Mother."

"No, but it's cloudy, and when I fed the chickens, there was a light mist."

"I'll wear my sweater," Janis said.

"Wonderful!" yelled Ellie. "Here, Wonderful!"

"Ellie," said Mrs. Huff, "stop that shrieking. If you aren't going to eat, go outside and gather the eggs."

A tear dribbled down Ellie's cheek as she took the basket her mother handed her. "Wonderful is lost," she said.

Mrs. Huff softened her voice and smiled as she added, "And then you can go down in the cellar and choose a jar of sauce to have with our noon meal."

Janis leaned close to Ellie and whispered,

"Look. Over there in the corner." She pointed. "Isn't that Wonderful's tail sticking out from behind the broom?"

Ellie looked where Janis pointed. Her eyes grew wide.

"Shh," Janis said. She held out her hand and Ellie took it. Together they tiptoed to the broom. When they were beside it, Janis grabbed the broom handle and lifted it into the air, exposing the empty corner.

"It's Wonderful!" cried Ellie. She dropped the egg basket, reached her hands toward the vacant space, and scooped the air toward her chest in a hug. "Naughty squirrel," she scolded. "You mustn't hide from me like that."

"Thank you, Janis," Mrs. Huff said. "Hurry now, or you'll be late for school."

"Goodbye, Mother," Janis said. "Goodbye, Ellie."

"Say goodbye to Wonderful," said Ellie.

"Goodbye, Wonderful," said Janis. She closed the door behind her and hurried across the farmyard past the chicken shed.

She ducked into the barn and slipped Pansy the apple she had packed in her lunch.

"I wish I didn't have to go to school today," Janis said as she gave Pansy one last pat.

21

But she knew she would push her father too far if she played hooky in order to stay with Pansy.

Fearful of what she might find when she came home, Janis walked out of the barn and headed up the road.

CHAPTER

4

"Ta-da!"

Warren Spalding placed a small wooden box on the worktable in his room at Gram's house. "The repair of the Instant Commuter is finished."

Betsy Tyler examined the box and nodded her approval. "Your grandpa was right when he said this machine is the most incredible invention of our time," she said. "It's more amazing than the Internet! More time-saving than frozen pizza!"

"This new box is sturdier than the first one was," Warren said. "There will be much less chance of damage to the Instant Commuter if it accidentally gets dropped."

Warren and Betsy stood at the worktable, beside the box. The Instant Commuter looked like an ordinary hinged box, except for a wire that came out of the bottom and was attached to a pencil-sized probe.

Betsy lifted the new box. "It isn't much heavier than the other box was," she said. She reached for the canvas backpack. "Do you want me to wear the Instant Commuter this time," she asked, "or do you want to wear it?"

"Let's do the trip tomorrow," Warren said.

"What's wrong with today? Everything's ready."

"I want to go over it all one more time," Warren said.

"We've been over everything a dozen times already," Betsy said. "I should think you would be eager to use the Instant Commuter again."

"I am. I just don't want any surprises, like I had when I thought I was going down the street to Pine Lake Middle School, and instead I went to Mount Saint Helens. *And* I went back to 1980, when the volcano was erupting."

"Now that we know the Instant Commuter

works on a photograph, as well as a map, we won't get in a mess like that again."

"I hope not," Warren said. "I still have nightmares about choking on volcanic ash."

"On that first trip we weren't prepared to travel through time. Now we are."

"I hope so."

"Our plan is foolproof," Betsy said. "I'll wear the Instant Commuter, and touch the probe to the photo of the blizzard. You hold on to me while we travel back in time to November 11, 1940."

"To Minnesota. To the blizzard of the century." Warren thought a moment. "Leave the Instant Commuter running, after we get there," he said, "in case we need to leave in a hurry."

"We won't need to leave in a hurry."

"It would be terrible to get stuck in 1940," Warren said. "They didn't even have television in 1940."

"We won't get stuck. We *will* get all the first-hand experience we need to write another A-plus report for Mr. Munson, and then we'll come back home. What could go wrong?"

"I don't know. That's what worries me. I've been reading about that blizzard. A freezing rain was followed by a record snowfall, and the storm caused one hundred and sixty-two deaths."

"It came up suddenly," Betsy said, "and people back in 1940 didn't have the kind of weather forecasts that we have now. People died because they weren't prepared. We are."

Warren said, "The temperature dropped below zero, and the wind gusted up to sixty miles per hour. The snow knocked out telephone and electrical lines; it was so deep that even the snowplows couldn't get through."

"Snow is sometimes colored," Betsy said. "It can be red, pink, yellow, or brown. Once in a while it's even green or blue. The coloring is caused by pollen or soot that collects on the ice crystals as they fall."

Warren sometimes kidded Betsy by calling her the Human Encyclopedia because she remembered so much odd information. Today he was in no mood to hear one of the strange facts that Betsy was always quoting. He was too nervous about taking another trip with the Instant Commuter.

When Warren first moved in with Gram for six months, while his mother finished college, he had been excited by the prospect of completing some of his late grandfather's inventions. Especially the Instant Commuter.

The lightweight machine was designed to be worn in a backpack. When the person wearing it touched the tip of the probe to a map, the person was transported to that place in less than one minute.

Grandpa had not realized that if the probe touched a photograph, the person was taken not only to the place in the photo, but to the time it was taken.

Warren found that out accidentally, which is how he had ended up fleeing for his life during the 1980 eruption of Mount Saint Helens.

After living through the volcano disaster, Warren was not going to take any chances with this blizzard. Not even to get an A on the report that he and Betsy were writing for their sixth-grade class on Natural Disasters.

"Let's look at the pictures again," Betsy said. "We never did decide exactly where we're going to go." She opened the library book that she and Warren had checked out, about the Armistice Day blizzard.

She turned to a photo of half a dozen cars buried almost to their rooftops in snow. Another picture showed workers shoveling snow out of the University of Minnesota football stadium.

Warren turned the page and gazed at a photo of dead hunters, found frozen near their duck blind. "I am not going there," he said.

"None of these pictures will work," Betsy said. "They were all taken after the storm, not during it."

She paged back to the front part of the book. "Here," she said, pointing to a blurry photo. "We could use this one."

Warren read the caption under the picture. "A farm in north central Minnesota. Photo taken by Janis Huff during the height of the storm."

"I wonder what she was trying to take a picture of," Betsy said.

"Whatever it was, it doesn't show."

"If we use this photo," Betsy said, "we'll land right in the middle of the blizzard. It will be perfect for our research."

"Maybe we should take a thermos of hot chocolate with us," Warren said.

"There isn't room in the backpack for anything but the Instant Commuter. And I want my hands free, so I can make notes."

"So do I."

"Besides, I do not plan to stay in the blizzard long enough to need hot chocolate," Betsy said. "We'll go there, look around to see what it was like, and come back. We'll only be gone about twenty minutes. Half an hour at the most."

Warren patted his shirt pocket. "I have the map of home, so we can return whenever we want to."

"Let's go now," Betsy said. "If we wait another day, we'll just get nervous."

"I'm already nervous."

"Nerve impulses in people can travel three hundred feet per second," Betsy said.

"Great," Warren said. "If my feet freeze, my brain will know immediately." He wondered if Betsy ever forgot anything she read or heard.

"Our feet are not going to freeze. If we get too cold, we can always return home for a while, and then make a second trip."

"One visit to a blizzard will be plenty for me," Warren said.

CHAPTER

5

Janis heard the clang of the brass school bell as she ran the last eighty rods toward the white wooden building. She rushed in the door and sat at her desk just as Miss Colby set the bell down and began to call the roll.

Janis answered, "Present," when she heard her name. She stood with the others and recited the Pledge of Allegiance. She turned to page 84 of her history book and tried to concentrate on what Miss Colby said about Thomas Jefferson. She heard Miss Colby talk about the war in Europe and say she hoped President Roosevelt would not let the United States get involved.

Through it all, Janis's thoughts were with Pansy. She wondered if Daddy was still thinking it over. She wondered if Pansy would be there when Janis got home from school. A tear leaked from Janis's eye, and she wiped it away with the back of her wrist.

When it was time for recess, Miss Colby said, "I want everyone to play outside during morning recess. We won't have many more fair days like this before winter arrives."

All the students stood up.

"Janis Huff," Miss Colby said, "please stay in. I want to talk to you. The rest of you are dismissed."

Janis blinked in surprise. The other students looked at her curiously for a moment before they spilled out the door into the school yard.

Janis walked to Miss Colby's desk. "Yes, Miss Colby?" she said.

"Is something wrong, Janis?" Miss Colby asked. "You seem distracted today. Unhappy. Not like yourself."

Janis hesitated for a moment.

"Anything you tell me will be confidential," Miss Colby said. "If you have a problem, perhaps I can help."

"Oh, Miss Colby," Janis said. "It's my

horse, Pansy. I've had her all my life and now she's gone blind and Daddy says he has to shoot her. I've begged him not to, but I'm afraid he'll do it anyway, while I'm at school."

Miss Colby stood, walked to Janis, and put an arm around her shoulders. "I'm so sorry," she said. "It's hard to lose an old friend."

"But I wouldn't *have* to lose her," Janis said. The tears began again. "Except for her eyesight, Pansy isn't sick at all. I can take care of her, if Daddy would just let me."

"I'm sure your father has good reason for his decision," Miss Colby said. "A horse eats a lot of grain and hay, especially in the winter months when it can't graze in the pasture."

"It isn't fair," Janis said. "Pansy's been a good worker, all these years. It isn't her fault she went blind."

Miss Colby was quiet for a moment. Then she said, "There are some things in life that, fair or not, we have to accept. The most we can do is to make the best of the situation." She handed Janis a handkerchief.

"If Daddy shoots Pansy," Janis said, "I'll never forgive him."

"I have an idea that might help a little," Miss Colby said.

The Blizzard Disaster

Janis waited.

Miss Colby pulled open the big bottom drawer of her desk and removed a camera. "My parents gave me this camera for my birthday," she said. "They want me to take pictures of our school, and of my pupils, and of the house where I'm boarding. When I go home to visit, I will be able to show them what my life is like here."

Janis looked curiously at the small black and silver camera.

"I want you to borrow this," Miss Colby said. "Take it home with you today and take a picture of Pansy. After I get the film developed, I'll give you the picture. That way you will always be able to remember your horse."

"I've never used a camera," Janis said. "We don't have one."

"It isn't hard." Miss Colby opened the top of the camera and let Janis look through the little window. She showed her how to aim; she pointed out the button to push, when Janis was ready to take her picture.

"Thank you, Miss Colby," Janis said. "I'll be very careful with your camera."

"I know you will," Miss Colby said. "You can return it to me tomorrow."

Janis nodded. She carried the camera to her

desk and laid it on the shelf beside her lunch. What she really wanted was to keep Pansy forever, but if she couldn't do that, at least she would have a picture of Pansy. It wasn't the same as having her horse, but it was something. And it was nice of Miss Colby to trust her with the camera.

Mother will be impressed, Janis thought, that I know how to use a camera. And Ellie will ask a million questions. She'll probably want me to take a picture of Wonderful.

Despite her worries, Janis smiled at the idea of taking a picture of an imaginary squirrel.

As Janis put the camera in her desk, the other students trooped back inside, shaking their heads and brushing drops of water off their clothing.

"The wind's come up," said Howard Drayford, one of the older boys. "And it's starting to sleet."

Miss Colby declared recess was over.

Janis tried to pay attention during spelling. She made herself listen as the two first grade students stumbled haltingly through their reading lesson. But part of her was already home, taking a picture of Pansy, and begging Daddy to wait awhile longer.

The Blizzard Disaster

Miss Colby looked out the window at noon and said, "It's snowing. We'll stay indoors to eat."

Janis had just finished her bread and syrup sandwich when Howard's father burst into the room. Before he could close the door, a flurry of snow followed him. Papers blew to the floor and the students scrambled to retrieve them.

"Sorry to interrupt like this, Miss Colby," Mr. Drayford said, "but there's a blizzard coming." He stamped his boots on the floor, knocking off big chunks of snow. "My neighbor heard on his radio that there's heavy snow and wind blowing in this afternoon. He called to warn me. I couldn't call here, so I came to tell you and to take Howard home."

Janis knew that Miss Colby had asked to have a telephone installed at the school, but it had not yet been done.

Miss Colby turned the knob on the school radio, and static filled the air. There were no stations close by, so reception was never strong, but sometimes she could bring in Station WCCO in Minneapolis. She fiddled with the dial.

Bits of a distant broadcast scratched over the airwaves. Janis recognized the voice of

35

Cedric Adams, but she could not make sense of what he was saying because his voice kept fading in and out. She did hear "all hotel rooms full" and "some telephone lines down."

Miss Colby shut the radio off and turned to Mr. Drayford.

"Do you think I should dismiss all of the children?" she asked.

"The way that wind is whipping around, these young ones should get home while they can still find the road. If it keeps snowing, the drifts will be deep. That's why I came for Howard as soon as I heard."

"I wonder if there's any danger in sending them home," Miss Colby said. "I'd rather they stayed here at school all night, if need be, than to have someone lost in a storm."

Howard's father thought for a moment. "A true blizzard could mean you'd be snowed in here for days, without food. Possibly without electricity. If telephone lines are down in the cities, our power lines may go down, too. I say send the children home, where their families can look after them."

Expectant faces looked at Miss Colby, hoping for the treat of an early dismissal.

"All right, children," Miss Colby said. "Get your coats."

"I didn't wear a coat," Lucille, one of the first graders said. "It wasn't cold this morning."

Miss Colby took her own sweater from its hook and put it on the child.

Lucille giggled and stuck her arms out to show everyone how the sleeves hung past her fingertips.

The rest of the students took their wraps from the hooks along one wall. Janis put her sweater on, wishing she had taken Mother's advice and worn her coat.

Thunk! The window shook, as if someone outside had thrown a big shovel full of snow at it.

"That wind is getting fierce," Mr. Drayford said.

"You are all to go straight home," Miss Colby said, "as fast as you can run. If you have a problem, and can't make it all the way home, go to the nearest house you can find and ask them to take you in."

"Come along, Howard," Mr. Drayford said. "Lucille, you come with me, too. And the Watson boys. I have room in the car, and your places are the same direction. I'll drop you at home and save your folks some worry."

"Thank you for coming to warn us, Mr. Drayford," Miss Colby said.

Janis was glad to see that Miss Colby had a lightweight coat in addition to the sweater she had given Lucille.

Janis clutched Miss Colby's camera in one hand. Mr. Drayford opened the door, and all fifteen students surged forward into the snowstorm.

The wind nearly took Janis's breath away, and the snow was already over the tops of her shoes. Some flakes were as big around as an egg.

"Run!" shouted Miss Colby from the doorway, and the students scattered like scared jackrabbits, each one racing toward home.

Janis lowered her head, envying her classmates who lived in the other direction. They had the wind at their backs. She had to go straight into it.

With her head down, snowflakes landed on the back of her neck. Janis shivered and turned up the collar of her dress.

There's one good thing about a snowstorm, she thought. Daddy won't have time to think about Pansy. He'll be too busy herding the cattle into shelter. As soon as I get home, I'll go in the barn and take my picture.

Holding the camera under her sweater so it wouldn't get wet, Janis plunged into the storm.

CHAPTER

6

Mr. Huff spent Monday morning mending fences, and trying to decide what to do about Pansy.

It began sleeting midmorning, and soon changed to snow, but bad weather had never kept Mr. Huff from his work. He went to the house for his knitted cap and his knee-high boots, and then continued to repair the downed fences.

As he looked for the last patch of broken fence on the east side of his land, he realized he could see only a few feet. Concerned about the cattle that were still out to pasture, he turned the truck toward home.

Mrs. Huff met him at the door. "It looks

bad," she said. "I tried to find the chickens, to put them in the henhouse, but some are still missing. It's hard to keep track of Ellie and hunt for chickens, too, when the snow is blowing every which way. We came back to get warm."

"I'm going out after the cattle," Mr. Huff said. "I came to get some gloves. Leave Ellie inside while you get the rest of the chickens."

"I want to help," Ellie said. "I want to go with you to find the cattle."

"You stay here in the kitchen," Mrs. Huff said as she pulled on a pair of overshoes, "and watch for Janis to come home. I'm sure Miss Colby will dismiss school early today."

"Janis can help me train Wonderful," Ellie said. "I'm teaching him to shake hands."

"Stay out of the cookies," Mrs. Huff said.

Snow swirled into the kitchen when Mr. and Mrs. Huff opened the door. Ellie went to the window and peered out. She saw her mother's green coat disappear into the whiteness.

Ellie pressed her nose against the cold windowpane. She heard the truck engine come to life, but all she saw through the thick, blowing snowflakes was the headlights as

Daddy drove toward the cornfield. Ellie was surprised that he took the truck. Usually, he would walk to the cornfield where the cattle were. He must be in a terrible hurry.

Ellie hoped Janis would get home soon. She didn't like to stay in the house by herself.

Warren and Betsy went down their check-list one last time, with Betsy reading the items aloud and Warren responding.

"Mittens," Betsy said.

"In our coat pockets."

"Matches."

"In my pocket." Warren put his hand in his pocket, to make sure the small box of wooden matches was there. It was.

"Hats." Betsy put one hand on top of her head and grinned at Warren. "You don't need to look," she said. "We're already wearing them."

"Right." He pulled his knitted stocking cap down over his ears. "I was letting my hair grow, to help keep my ears warm," he said, "but Gram made me get it cut yesterday. She said she couldn't see my eyes."

"Speaking of hair in your eyes," Betsy said, "I got a new foster dog last night, from the

Purebred Dog Rescue. He's an Old English sheepdog."

"They're big, aren't they?" Warren asked.

"Huge. He's only six months old, and he already weighs more than seventy pounds. His paws are the size of grapefruit."

"I'll help you walk him," Warren said.

"Good. It may take both of us. Mongo needs some obedience training."

Warren had helped Betsy walk her last foster dog, a Welsh corgi that she had cared for until the Purebred Dog Rescue found a good home for Creampuff.

"Where did Mongo come from?" Warren asked.

"The county animal shelter."

"He's a stray?"

Betsy shook her head. "His owners turned him in because he got too big. Can you believe it? They buy a purebred Old English sheepdog puppy, and then they're surprised when he turns out to be larger than a toy poodle. Honestly, people can be so stupid sometimes."

Warren had learned to be quiet when Betsy got started about irresponsible pet owners. Although he agreed with everything she said,

43

it seemed to make her even more angry if he responded to her tirades.

"If they want a small dog, fine," Betsy said. "But why do they choose a puppy that's clearly identified as being a large breed? Did they really think he was going to stay a puppy his whole life?"

Betsy glared at Warren as if he had turned the Old English sheepdog in to the animal shelter.

Warren decided it would be best to change the subject. "What's after hats?" he asked. "On the checklist?"

Betsy blinked at him, as if trying to remember what checklist he might be talking about. Then she looked at the paper she held in her hand and said, "Boots."

"Check," said Warren. "On our feet."

"Map of home."

"In my pocket."

"Coats."

"Ready to be put on."

"That's it," said Betsy. "Let's do it."

She put on her heavy winter coat and zipped up the front. She pulled her stocking cap over her ears.

Meanwhile, Warren put the Instant Commuter in the backpack, with the probe hanging out the special opening in the bottom.

While Warren put on his coat, Betsy put the backpack on and buckled the chest strap, so there was no chance of the backpack accidentally slipping off.

Warren took the rectangular piece of green plastic that he had cut from a large garbage bag and pinned one corner to each of the backpack's shoulder straps. The plastic bag hung down over the backpack.

"I feel like Batman, wearing a green cape," Betsy said.

"This will ensure that the Instant Commuter stays dry. I'm not taking any chance of not coming straight home from this trip."

Betsy gripped the probe firmly in her right hand. "Ready?"

"Ready."

She hesitated. "You want to hear something odd?" she said.

Betsy was always quoting strange facts, but Warren could hardly believe she would do it now, right when they were about to take off on a trip backward in time.

"What?" he said.

"I'm jittery."

"You are?" That was a surprise.

Betsy nodded. "I'm the one who talked you into going to see the blizzard for ourselves before we write the report, but now that it's time to leave, I'm kind of scared."

"We don't have to go," Warren said.

"Oh, I still want to go. I just didn't expect to be nervous."

"If we weren't a little apprehensive, there would be something wrong with our heads," Warren said.

"Are you scared, too?"

"I'm terrified."

Betsy beamed at him. "Oh, good," she said. "That makes me feel better."

She reached over her shoulder and turned the Instant Commuter on. "Grab hold," she said.

Warren stood behind Betsy. He put his arms firmly around her waist, feeling the hard Instant Commuter box against his chest. He smelled the wool of her stocking cap. He watched over her shoulder as Betsy pointed the probe at the blurry photo of the blizzard.

She tapped the tip down in the center of the picture. As soon as the probe hit the photo, the Instant Commuter began its low hum, and Warren could feel a breeze blow across his room.

The Blizzard Disaster

Warren had spent several hours trying to adjust the controls so that the breeze would be less like a hurricane. He realized his efforts had not worked.

The breeze quickly became a full-blown wind; Betsy clung to the edge of the table, and Warren clasped his hands tightly together in front of Betsy's jacket.

Both kids closed their eyes and waited to see where they would be when they stopped. If their plan worked, they would be in Minnesota on November 11, 1940.

CHAPTER

7

Janis's feet felt like blocks of ice. She knew she should never have started for home wearing only ankle socks and oxfords on her feet.

She should not have started for home at all; she should have stayed at school. It would be better to go without food for a few days than to freeze to death alone in a blizzard.

Her ears and nose were so numb she wasn't sure they were still attached to her head. She still held Miss Colby's camera; it felt frozen to her hand.

She stuck her other hand in her armpit, to try to warm it. Her fingers were so cold they felt brittle, as if they would snap off at the slightest bump.

Snowbanks, like giant marshmallows, formed beside her. Then, in the blowing wind, they shifted, broke up, and formed again on her other side, bigger than before.

The snow came up to her knees now and she was weary from the effort of lifting her legs to step forward.

Janis forced herself to keep moving. Sharp pains shot down her legs with every step. She was no longer certain she was going in the right direction. It seemed hours since she had left the school, and she had not yet passed the Wilsons' place, which was nearly a mile before her own farm.

If I do see the Wilsons', she decided, I'll go there. They'll take me in and I can call Mother and Daddy to let them know where I am. But was she near the Wilsons'? Was she still on the road?

The wind died down for a moment, and Janis heard a different sound. She recognized the hum of the telephone wires. If I follow the telephone lines, she thought, I'll stay on the road. The humming will lead me.

Now that she was aware of the sound, she could make it out even when the wind picked up again. Feeling encouraged, Janis concentrated on the humming noise and kept moving.

Once, as she pushed her way through a snowbank, the wind suddenly blew the snow away, and Janis fell face forward onto the bare road.

Instinctively she stuck her hands out to brace herself. When she landed, her finger snapped the shutter on Miss Colby's camera. The howling wind was so loud that Janis did not realize she had just taken her first photograph.

The camera was jarred out of her hand and bounced into the snowbank.

Janis got to her knees, feeling frantically in the snow for the camera. She had not seen where it went, and now she stuck her bare hands deep into the drifts, feeling with her fingers for the small metal case. She did not find it.

I'll have to leave it, she thought, and go on.

By then, the wind had shifted and the road was again covered with snow. I won't have a picture of Pansy now, Janis thought. And how will I replace Miss Colby's camera?

Some drifts reached her waist, and Janis's strength dwindled. Maybe Daddy would hitch

The Blizzard Disaster

Jupiter and Pansy to the wagon and come to get her. She knew the truck would never get through these drifts, but the horses might be able to, especially if they were both hitched and pulling together.

Was Pansy still alive, Janis wondered, to help pull the wagon? Janis knew that if Daddy decided to follow through on his decision to end Pansy's life, he would do it while Janis was in school. He would not want her to hear the shot, or to see the horse go down.

She didn't *want* to see it, or hear it. But it was almost as terrible not to know—to wonder what was happening, to imagine the worst, and not be sure.

Tears formed in Janis's eyes—tears for Pansy and tears for herself. She knew she was in as much danger of death this day as her horse was.

The tears froze in the corners of Janis's eyes before they could run down her face.

She remembered Miss Colby telling the students about a blizzard in 1888 where people froze to death only a few yards from buildings where they could have sought shelter. Because they could not see the buildings, the people never knew how close they were.

Miss Colby said those who survived the

blizzard went out at daybreak on the day after the storm, to search for bodies and take them in before the wolves ate them.

"NO!" Janis shouted. The howling wind blew the word back into her face.

Mr. Huff hoped he was steering toward where he had last seen the cattle, but it was impossible to tell for sure. It was like driving into a huge ball of cotton; the only thing he saw in the headlights was snow.

The truck stopped moving. He got out, intending to shovel a path for a few feet in front of the tires, just enough to get started again. When he stepped out, he sank to his knees in a drift, and he knew there was no way he would get the truck through.

He would have to find the cattle on foot.

A farmer all his life, Mr. Huff was not easily daunted by weather, or anything else. But as he struggled forward through the drifts, he realized he might not find the cattle. And if he did find them, he was no longer sure he would be able to drive them home to shelter. He could lose all forty head to this storm, a loss Mr. Huff could not afford.

The wind drove the cold clear through him. Ice particles pelted his face, making it hard to keep his eyes open. His neck felt rubbed raw where his coat collar chafed against his wet skin. Still he fought his way forward.

If the cattle died, he would be unable to pay off the bank loan he had used to buy them. Instead of earning a profit from raising them, he would have a loss. Where would he get the money? How would he feed his family?

An odd tinkling noise came from his left; Mr. Huff turned in that direction. He heard the noise again. It sounded like glass breaking.

"Hello!" he called. "Is someone there?"

The tinkling and crackling grew louder, rising above the wind.

Mr. Huff followed the noise and then stopped, stunned, as he reached its source. It was part of his herd—fifteen or twenty cows—all of them so covered with ice that it rattled and cracked when they moved.

The cattle had traveled away from the wind and were now huddled against the fence, unable to go farther. Their tails, caked with ice, stuck out sideways when the wind caught them.

As he approached, one of the cows fell over. Mr. Huff rushed to her side. The cow thrashed in the snow, and Mr. Huff realized she couldn't breathe.

He grabbed the cow around the neck, forcing her head to be still while he used his bare hands to pry the ice from her nostrils. His hands had enough warmth to melt the ice so that he could get it out.

Once the chunks of ice were gone, the frightened cow got up again. Another minute, Mr. Huff knew, and that cow would have suffocated.

Mr. Huff squeezed around the cows until he had the fence at his back. The most direct route home would be diagonally across the field, but the safest way would be to follow the fence line east until he hit the road. He decided to be safe.

"Hey, there!" he shouted. He clapped his hands, urging the cows to move forward along the fence. "Go, Bossie!" he yelled. "Back to your barn."

The confused cattle moved away from him for a short distance, but turned back when the wind blew in their faces.

"Hey, girl. Go on now!" Mr. Huff yelled. He ran back and forth as fast as he could move in the deep drifts, trying to herd the cattle forward. Slowly they moved away from him, following the fence line.

Finding the cows gave Mr. Huff fresh energy, and he waved his arms over his head, yelling as he urged the frightened beasts to keep moving. Jumping back and forth to keep the cattle together kept Mr. Huff's blood flowing so that his feet didn't feel quite as frozen as they had earlier.

"Keep going!" he shouted. "Move along, now. Move on!"

The cattle milled restlessly forward, with the ice on their bodies still crackling as they moved.

A mile away, on the other side of the fence, Janis struggled on through waist-high drifts. The frigid air hurt her chest when she inhaled.

Usually, she could walk home from school in less than forty minutes. She wasn't sure how much time had passed since she left the school today. It seemed like hours. Was it getting dark, or was the snow so thick it only seemed like nighttime? She felt stranded in a sea of snow.

She knew she had to keep moving. If she didn't, she would surely freeze.

Twice, when she felt she could not bear the wind on her face another second, she stopped briefly and turned her back to the storm.

The wind swirled around her, lifting her hair and pushing snowflakes under her collar. For a time, the wind gusted so hard that snow blew right through the loose knitting of Janis's sweater.

She wondered what Mother and Daddy were doing. Were they out looking for her? No, she thought, Mother would stay home with Ellie and keep a fire going and a pot of soup.

But Daddy would look for her; she was certain of that. Unless, of course, Daddy had been caught in the blizzard, too.

CHAPTER

8

Mrs. Huff put the last of the firewood in the cookstove.

"Look!" Ellie called from the living room. "It's snowing inside the house."

Mrs. Huff's heart sank as she saw snow creep across the living-room linoleum, blown in through the cracks around the windows. It was coming under the door, too, forming a small drift. It even blew through the keyhole.

Mrs. Huff hurried upstairs and pulled the heavy wool blanket from her bed. She got a hammer and nails, and hung the blanket across the opening from the kitchen to the living room.

"We're going to stay in the kitchen," she

told Ellie. "The blanket will keep the heat in there."

"Wonderful wants to play in the snow on the floor," Ellie said.

"Wonderful can play in the snow," Mrs. Huff replied. "You and I are going in the kitchen."

"When will Janis get home?" Ellie said.

Mrs. Huff pressed her lips together and hugged herself to keep her fears inside. "Soon, I hope," she said. "And your father, too." She peered out the window for the twentieth time, hoping to see something besides snow. Hoping to see something alive.

Worries fluttered around her brain like moths at the barn light. What will I do if Luke doesn't get here soon? Why didn't we cut and stack the firewood sooner? How will we survive if the cattle are gone?

And the worst, most awful worry of them all: Where is Janis? Is she safe at school—or is she lost in this terrible storm?

Mrs. Huff lifted the telephone receiver, to call Mrs. Wilson at the next farm over. Maybe Janis was there. She heard nothing.

"The telephone's out," she said.

"Wonderful!" said Ellie, lifting up the bottom of the blanket and looking into the living room. "Here, Wonderful!"

"Put the blanket down," Mrs. Huff said. "You're letting heat out of the kitchen."

"I have to go get Wonderful. He'll be cold in there."

"Oh, for heaven's sake, Ellie," Mrs. Huff said. "This is not the time for games."

"It isn't a game," Ellie insisted. "I need to bring Wonderful into the kitchen."

Mrs. Huff stared out the window, shivering in spite of the sweater she wore. It was growing cold, even here in the kitchen. She opened the cookstove door and stirred the fire. The last log crumbled into charred pieces and settled on the ash that covered the bottom of the firebox.

She remembered that Janis and Ellie had gathered twigs for kindling. She opened the kitchen door and stepped out into the storm, feeling in the snow with her bare hands until she found the apple basket. She brought the basket of twigs into the kitchen and used a towel to brush the snow off them.

Not bothering to mop up the snow before it could melt into puddles on the floor, she threw a handful of twigs into the remains of the fire. They were too damp to catch quickly, but they smoldered and smoked, and eventually went up in quick little bursts of flame.

The twigs were too small to generate much heat, but they kept the fire from going out completely. When the first batch of sticks died down, she threw in a few more, and a few more, until the basket was empty.

In less than twenty minutes, she thought, I've used up a month's worth of future kindling. But I can't let the fire die. Without it, Ellie and I will freeze. And she needed a warm kitchen for Janis and Luke to come home to.

She looked around the room, wondering what she could burn. The wood box, she thought, as her eyes stopped at the old wooden box with slatted sides that stood between the stove and the cellar door. In winter, the Huffs kept the box filled with firewood, so that they didn't have to go outside every time they needed another log.

If she could pry the sides off the wood box, she could break up the individual slats and make them short enough to fit in the stove. She opened the tool drawer, removed the hammer, and began pounding on the inside of the wooden box.

The third time the hammer smashed into the box, the side splintered.

Stunned by her mother's destruction, Ellie said, "You wrecked it."

Jagged pieces of wood stuck out from the box, and Mrs. Huff used the claw end of the hammer to pry them off. One at a time she fed them into the fire. They were as dry as dust, and the fire quickly flared up after each addition.

But it burned down again far too soon after it blazed up.

While Mrs. Huff concentrated on dismantling the wooden box that usually held their firewood, Ellie stuck her head under the blanket and peeked in the other room. She did not see Wonderful anywhere. She hoped he had not gone outside when she wasn't looking. It was much too cold out, even for a squirrel in a fur coat.

Mrs. Huff watched the last of the wooden box burn down to embers. Then, with tears in her eyes, she tried to break the legs off one of the kitchen chairs. The chairs had been hers ever since her marriage, and her mother's before that. Mrs. Huff remembered sitting on those chairs as a child, eating toast and eggs while her mother sang in the kitchen.

And her own children, her darling Janis and dear little Ellie, had eaten every meal of their young lives on those very same chairs. Mrs. Huff did not want to burn them, but if it was a choice between burning her mother's chairs and letting her family freeze, the chairs would have to go.

Janis! she thought. Where are you? Where is Luke? Oh, please, dear God, keep my family safe.

As if in answer to her prayer, the kitchen door flew open and Mr. Huff, covered from head to toe with ice and snow, staggered into the room. Ice hung from his eyebrows. His cheeks were white from frostbite. Even his eyes looked white.

Ellie stood with her back to the blanket and yelled, "Mommy!"

Mrs. Huff gasped and ran to him. She scraped the ice from the buttons on his coat and helped him get the coat off. When she set the coat on the floor, it was so rigid that it stood upright by itself.

Fascinated, Ellie crept closer to look at it.

"Red ice!" cried Ellie. "Look, there's red ice on Daddy's coat."

"Don't touch it!" Mrs. Huff snapped. "It's blood from Daddy's neck. The wet wool chafed him that much."

Subdued, Ellie sat on the floor and stared at the coat.

"I g-g-got f-f-fifteen head of c-c-attle b-back into the b-barn," Mr. Huff said. It was hard for Mrs. Huff and Ellie to understand his words because his teeth chattered so hard. He stood close to the cookstove, rubbing his hands together over the meager heat.

Mrs. Huff took the teakettle that she had kept on top of the stove and filled her dishpan with water. She tested it, to be sure it wasn't too hot. She helped her husband remove his boots and his stiff, frozen socks. He eased his feet into the water.

Mrs. Huff ladled pea soup into a cup and held it to his lips. He sipped it gratefully.

"Did Janis get home?" he asked when he could talk again.

"No. And the telephone is out so I don't know if she's at the Wilsons'."

"Perhaps Miss Colby kept everyone at school," Mr. Huff said.

"I hope so. It was all I could do to catch the chickens and get them in the coop. When

Janis didn't come, I didn't dare take Ellie and set out to look for her."

"You did right," Mr. Huff said. "I wasn't sure I was going to make it back with those cattle. As it is, I lost a few head somewhere in the cornfield."

"We're out of firewood," Mrs. Huff said. "I've already burned the twigs that the girls had gathered for kindling. I burned the wood box, too."

Mr. Huff reached for a towel and began drying his feet. "There's some chopped wood by the henhouse," he said. "I cut it this morning. Didn't like being down to our last wood-box full."

"I'll bring it in," Mrs. Huff said. "You can't go back out this soon."

"You'll never find it, under the snow. I didn't stack it because I planned to have Janis do it when she got home from school. I'll go get it; I know exactly where it is."

Mrs. Huff left the kitchen and hurried upstairs to get him some dry socks.

His fingers were still so stiff that he was unable to put them on alone.

"Wear your work shoes," she said. "Those boots are covered with ice. And here's a dry pair of gloves."

The Blizzard Disaster

There wasn't any choice but to put on the same coat; it was the only heavy coat Mr. Huff had. Mrs. Huff used her broom to knock the ice from it before she held it up and he stuck his arms into the frozen sleeves.

"I think Wonderful went outside," Ellie said.

Her parents ignored her. Mrs. Huff brushed the last of the ice off Mr. Huff's hat and handed it to him. He put it on.

Mr. Huff plunged out the door. Five minutes later he returned, dumping an armload of logs onto the kitchen floor. Mrs. Huff quickly grabbed two of them and stuffed them into the wood stove. Ice on the bark sizzled and spit, and for a moment she feared she had put the fire out. But the wood caught, and by the time Mr. Huff returned with a second load, the kitchen was warm again.

He made three trips, bringing back as much wood as he could carry each time. On the third trip he let go of the wood and then dropped to his knees.

"That will see us through the night," Mrs. Huff said. "You're exhausted." Again, she helped him remove his coat, gloves, and shoes. She refilled the pan with warm water. Mr. Huff sat down and gratefully put his feet in the water. "I have never," he said, "been so tired, or so cold."

"Now that you're back," Mrs. Huff said, "I'm going to walk a bit and call for Janis. It's possible she's nearby and can't see the house."

Mr. Huff looked at his wife and saw his own deepest fears reflected in her expression. He nodded. "Get the clothesline," he said. "We'll tie it to the doorknob, and you can hold the other end in your hand, to be sure you can find your way back."

"Is Janis lost in the blizzard?" Ellie asked.

"We hope not," Mr. Huff said. "But we can't know for sure."

"I want to go look for Janis," Ellie said.

"You are going to stay here, where it's warm," Mrs. Huff said.

"I never get to go," Ellie said. "Wonderful is lost in the blizzard, too. I want to look for Wonderful."

"Hush, Ellie," Mrs. Huff said. "We have enough trouble without listening to you complain."

Ellie watched as her mother pulled on an extra pair of heavy socks. Next Mrs. Huff put on her high boots, and wound a blue scarf around her nose and mouth. With her coat collar turned up, and her wool hat pulled down as far as it would go, all Ellie could see of her mother's face was her eyes.

Mr. Huff took his feet out of the water and walked to the telephone, leaving wet foot-prints on the floor. He picked up the receiver, listened, and put it down. "Still dead," he said. "When you get too cold, come back. By then I'll be warmed and ready to look for her myself."

"You're in no condition to go out again," Mrs. Huff replied.

"Whatever you do," Mr. Huff said, "don't let go of the rope. The snow is blowing so hard, it will blind you."

"Like Pansy?" Ellie said. "Was Pansy in a blizzard?"

Mr. Huff did not answer Ellie's question. He watched his wife carry the clothesline across the cold living room and out the door. He listened to the rattle of the doorknob as her fingers fumbled to tie a knot. He didn't like having his wife go out into the blizzard while he stayed inside, but he knew he had to get warm, and get his strength back before he ventured out again.

He returned to the kitchen and finished his cup of soup. Then he dumped the dishpan of water into the sink and refilled the pan with hot water. He stuck his feet in and sat as close to the stove as he could get. He didn't think he would ever stop shaking.

Ellie peeked into the living room again. She could no longer see out the windows because so much snow had blown in between the storm windows and the regular glass that the entire window looked white.

Ellie scowled at the cold, empty living room. She didn't like this old blizzard. Mother and Daddy didn't pay any attention to her, and Janis didn't come home, and she didn't want to stay in the kitchen.

Where was Wonderful? What if Wonderful turned blind from being in this storm? Everyone was worried about Janis being out in the storm, but nobody cared that Wonderful was also missing.

I'll have to find him myself, she decided. She climbed the stairs to her bedroom and found last year's snowboots in the closet. When she tried to put them on, they were too small. No matter how hard she shoved her feet into them, she couldn't make them fit.

She put her shoes back on. She didn't know

how to tie them; usually Janis did that for her.

She found her winter coat, hanging on a hook in the back of her closet. She found an old straw hat, too, but she didn't know where her mittens were.

Ellie went back downstairs. She ducked around the curtain and went into the kitchen, intending to ask Daddy to tie her shoes for her. When she saw him, she stopped.

Daddy's head had drooped to his chest, and she could tell from his deep, even breathing that he had fallen asleep. She didn't want to wake him up to tie her shoes.

Mother had gone out the living-room door, toward the road. Ellie decided to go out the kitchen door. She would look for Wonderful up in the chestnut tree, and she could look for Janis in the barn. Janis was probably sitting in that old barn with Pansy, the way she had all weekend.

Ellie pulled the door open and stepped outside, shocked by how cold it was. Quickly she shut the door behind her.

Bits of ice stung her face.

Ellie held her hat on with one hand. Janis isn't wearing a coat, she thought. Wonderful doesn't have a coat, either. It was up to Ellie to find them.

"Wonderful!" she called as she started toward the barn. "Here, Wonderful!"

It was hard to see. Ellie wondered how white snow could make the world look dark. She wished she had her mittens.

Ellie stuck her cold hands deep in her pockets. The instant she let go of her hat, the wind snatched it and sailed it high over the chicken shed.

For a moment Ellie hesitated, wondering if she should go back inside. But what about Janis? And Wonderful? Determined, Ellie put her head down and pushed her small body forward through the drifts.

In seconds the wind covered her tracks.

CHAPTER

9

On their first trip with the Instant Commuter, Warren and Betsy had felt a strong wind during the travel time. The wind had stopped when they arrived at their destination.

On this trip the wind didn't stop. Instead, it blew harder, and colder. They opened their eyes to snow, hurtling straight at them. The wind ripped the garbage bag cape from Betsy's shoulders; it flapped away like a huge green bird.

Warren let go of Betsy and looked around. Snowdrifts, like huge mounds of mashed potatoes, rose on every side.

"It worked," Warren said. "Welcome to 1940."

Betsy moved away from him, heading into the storm.

"Wait for me," Warren said. "We need to stay together."

"I thought I saw something move," Betsy said. "Over this way."

She lunged forward into a snowdrift, with Warren right behind her. When they had gone about ten feet, Betsy stopped. "I guess I was wrong," she said. "There isn't anyone here."

"Let's keep moving," Warren said. "We aren't going to last long in this, if we don't keep moving."

"We won't last long, period," Betsy said. "I've never seen so much snow. I intended to take notes, but the paper would blow out of my hands. Besides, I don't want to take off my mittens in order to use a pencil."

"I wonder what the windchill factor is."

"I don't think they knew about windchill in 1940," Betsy said.

Warren led the way, lifting his knees almost to his chest in order to get his feet far enough above the snow to move them forward. Betsy stayed close behind him, so that Warren acted as a snowplow, clearing a path for her. After a few minutes they traded positions, and Betsy went first.

The Blizzard Disaster

They did not try to talk. Both were paying attention to details that they would be able to use in their report: the hard, frozen ground underfoot, slippery beneath the new snow; the way the wind whipped the top layer of snow back into the air so that each flake seemed to fall more than once; the bitter sting of the icy crystals against their cheeks.

Most of all, they were aware of a total isolation from the rest of the world. They could see no buildings, no lights, and no people. They heard no traffic noise. There was only the frigid blinding whiteness, surrounding them.

Before she came to the end of the clothesline, Mrs. Huff knew it was useless to search for Janis on foot. It had taken her at least half an hour just to reach the road. Her hands and feet ached from the cold, and her breath had frozen on the blue scarf, covering it with so much ice that she had to pull it below her nose in order to breathe.

"Janis!" she shouted, before she turned back.

Janis is a smart girl, Mrs. Huff told herself as she fought her way back to the house, going hand over hand along the clothesline.

Janis would know enough to go to the Wilsons' house and stay with them. Maybe she had not started home, at all. She was probably warm and snug in the schoolhouse with Miss Colby, telling stories by the fire.

Mr. Huff woke with a start when Mrs. Huff clattered into the kitchen, stomping her boots and shaking her blue scarf over the cookstove so that the clumps of snow fell off and sizzled like sausages until they turned to steam.

"Any sign of her?" he asked.

"No." Mrs. Huff rubbed her red hands over the stove while Mr. Huff put another log on the fire. "I couldn't see more than two feet in front of my face. Without the clothesline, I might not have made it back." Her tired legs trembled; she sat beside the stove. She told herself that Janis was safe, either at school or at a neighboring farm. She had to believe that; to believe anything else was too horrible.

Mr. Huff pulled on his heavy boots once more. "I'm going to hitch up Jupiter and Pansy to the old wagon," he said. "They may be able to break through the drifts."

"Oh, Luke, are you sure? Janis may be safe at the school all along."

"And she may be partway home," Mr. Huff said. "I have to try. I should have done this sooner, instead of looking for the cattle, but I thought Janis would be home when I got here."

"If Janis started out in this storm," Mrs. Huff said slowly, "it may be too late to look for her." Her eyes filled with tears, but she forced herself to continue. "I don't want to lose both of you."

"If I don't find her between here and the Wilsons' place, I'll give up. I'll come home and wait until the blizzard ends."

While he put on his hat and gloves, Mrs. Huff held his heavy jacket open, with the inside facing the hot stove. He slid his arms into the sleeves. "I wish it would stay that warm the whole time I have it on," he said.

"Be careful," she said. "Use the clothesline from here to the barn."

"Keep the fire going, and try not to worry."

"Hurry," she said.

After he left, she ladled soup into a cup and sipped it, savoring the warmth as it slid down her throat. "Ellie?" she said. "Do you want some soup?"

When Ellie didn't answer, Mrs. Huff looked under the table, and behind the curtain that hung from the sink, where Ellie often played. "Ellie? Where are you? Ellie, answer me!"

The wind rattled the windowpane. A frozen branch scratched the side of the house like a long, icy finger.

"Ellie, are you in the living room, playing in the snow?" Mrs. Huff walked across the kitchen and jerked aside the blanket. She searched quickly through the living room and then ran upstairs to Ellie's bedroom.

"Ellie!" she called. "If you're hiding, you come out this minute."

Ellie's bed was empty. But the closet door stood open and Ellie's snowboots from last year lay on the floor beside the bed. Mrs. Huff picked them up. Those boots had not been out of the closet since last March. Had Ellie found them and tried to put them on?

Why? Fear made Mrs. Huff's heart race. She reached into the closet and pushed Ellie's summer clothes to one side. She looked at the hook where Ellie's heavy coat had hung. The hook was empty.

"No," Mrs. Huff whispered to the empty room. "Oh, dear God, please, please no."

She rushed through the other two bedrooms, calling frantically. Finding no sign of Ellie, she ran back downstairs.

She pulled the living-room door open and hollered into the storm. "Ellie! Are you out there? Come this way! Come home!"

Her only answer was the wind, blowing more snow into the house. She slammed the door shut.

At least Ellie had worn a warm coat. Mrs. Huff tried to find comfort in that.

I'll have to go out again, Mrs. Huff thought. She tried to think where Ellie might go but quickly realized it didn't matter, because Ellie would be lost as soon as she got ten feet from the house.

As Mrs. Huff hurried back to the kitchen, to put her coat back on, the lights went out. She fumbled in a drawer until she found a candle and matches. When the candle was lit, she could see to light the oil lamp.

She grabbed her coat, which was still covered with ice, and put it back on.

Holding the lamp chest high, she stepped out the kitchen door. She stood, shivering, with her back to the door, and screamed Ellie's name into the storm.

When there was no answer, she went inside and put the lamp on the window ledge, where its light could be seen from outdoors. Then she went out and, keeping one hand on the

77

siding, walked around the house, calling Ellie's name, over and over.

The clothesline was still tied to the doorknob. She decided to follow it to the barn. Perhaps she could reach Luke before he started off with Jupiter and Pansy. He could help her search their own property before he set off toward the Wilsons'. Mrs. Huff felt certain that Ellie would not have gone far.

Grasping the clothesline, she walked as far as she could. Twice her legs buckled, dropping her suddenly into snow over her head. Each time it was harder to get back on her feet. She shouted until she was too hoarse to call any more.

The clothesline did not stretch all the way to the barn. When she reached the end, she returned to the house and went inside.

She yearned to keep going, to look everywhere, but she knew she could not. She was too tired and too cold; if she set out now she would never make it home. Luke and Janis and, she hoped, Ellie would return and find her frozen body in the field.

Feeling sick to her stomach, Mrs. Huff sank onto a chair. Why didn't I look for her as soon as I got back? she thought. How could I have talked about the blizzard, and warmed Luke's coat, and poured soup without noticing that my child was missing?

She wondered how long Ellie had been gone. Luke had probably fallen asleep and Ellie felt neglected. It wasn't Luke's fault; she knew that. He was exhausted from driving the cattle home, and Ellie often played out of sight—under the table or sink, or behind the wood box—with her doll or her "squirrel."

If Ellie had asked permission, Luke would never have allowed her to leave the house. No doubt Ellie decided to find out for herself what a blizzard was like. Or maybe she was looking for that nonexistent squirrel again.

Whatever the reason, Ellie was gone.

CHAPTER

10

The hum of the telephone wires stopped.

Janis stopped to catch her breath, willing the wind to die down for a moment so she could hear better. She had followed the hum for a long ways—a quarter of a mile perhaps—and it had given her hope that she would survive.

As long as she heard the humming, she knew she was moving toward a house. It didn't matter if it was her own home or a neighbor's or a total stranger's. Any house where she could get in out of the cold would be fine.

The humming did not return. Did I go the wrong way? she wondered. Did I walk away from the telephone lines without knowing it?

She took a few steps backward, but she still heard only the howling of the wind.

She tried going to her right but stopped after only a few feet. I can't do this, she thought. If I'm not already lost, I will be if I start going in different directions. Some of the phone lines probably blew down, or got so heavy with ice that they collapsed.

The wind had been in her face when she left the school, and she had kept the wind in her face ever since. Unless the wind had shifted, that meant she had been going south all this time. If she kept going south, she would eventually be home.

Of course, it would be easy to miss the house. It was far enough back from the road that she would not be able to see it. But surely, she would see something she recognized—the mailbox at the end of the drive, or the chestnut tree near the ditch—some landmark that would alert her to turn.

Her legs felt like fence posts. Forcing her feet to lift up and go down again, Janis stumbled on.

Ellie decided that Wonderful must have stayed inside, after all. It was too cold out, and Wonderful didn't like to be alone in the dark. Ellie turned around, to go home.

Her teeth chattered and her hands hurt. Her feet ached, too. She wished she had her boots on, even if they were too tight. Snow drifted as high as Ellie's chest, and she couldn't see which way to go.

She pushed her way through the drift, but when she emerged, the wind caught her and blew her over onto her back. She flailed her arms and kicked her feet. This wasn't fun, like making snow angels. She sank deeper into the snow.

Panicked, Ellie screamed for help. "Daddy! Daddy, help me!"

Why didn't Daddy come?

She screamed again and then the horrible realization hit her that Daddy could not hear her. He was inside, with the door shut, and he didn't know she was out here. No one knew she was out here.

Ellie pulled her knees toward her chest and rocked back onto her shoulders. Then she flung her head forward, and rolled over, somersaulting out of the snowbank.

The wind threw tiny pieces of ice at Ellie's face. It was too hard, going that direction. She would go a different way. She would look for the barn. Maybe she would sit in the barn with Pansy, the way Janis liked to do.

Ellie turned her back to the wind. She wasn't sure where the barn was, but she thought she was almost there.

Ellie wished she had stayed next to the warm cookstove, as Mother had told her to do. The snow was up to her chin in places and it took all of Ellie's strength to labor onward.

She pushed her way into one drift after another, shaking with cold and fear. As she stepped forward into yet another mound of snow, her foot went down, and down, beyond where the ground should have been.

Ellie tumbled forward into the ditch that ran alongside the road. She lay still, too frightened and weary to get up.

Mr. Huff put blankets on Jupiter and Pansy, securing them around the middle with rope. He hitched the horses to the old wagon and urged them out into the storm.

They fought their way through the drifts, until they found what Mr. Huff hoped was the road. Instinctively the two horses turned north, so the wind was at their backs, and Mr. Huff let them go, knowing that was the direction of the school.

It was slow going, even with both horses. Hoping a lighter load would help, Mr. Huff jumped down and walked alongside, holding on to Jupiter's bridle. But he did not have enough strength left in his legs to walk far in the deep snow, and he soon climbed back onto the wagon.

"Janis!" Mr. Huff shouted, over and over. "Janis, can you hear me?" His only answer was the wailing wind.

The horses stopped. No amount of urging could make them continue. Mr. Huff got down again and fought his way to Jupiter's head. The snowbank in front of the horses came up to their chests. It was impossible for them to pull the wagon any farther.

Mr. Huff tugged on Jupiter's bridle, trying to lead the horses in a circle and turn the wagon around. That was impossible, too. The snow beside them was as deep as the drifts in front of them, and the wagon was too large to turn easily.

They were stuck.

I'll have to turn the animals loose, Mr. Huff thought, and hope they can somehow find their way back. I'll ride Jupiter, to make sure he keeps moving. If he makes it home, I will, too.

He unhitched both horses. He led Pansy away from the wagon, forcing his way through the deep drift, and let her reins drop into the snow.

He pulled on Jupiter's bridle until he got the horse turned around. Jupiter struggled, not wanting to head into the wind.

Mr. Huff grasped Jupiter's mane and, clinging with his frozen fingers, managed to hoist himself aboard the horse. Again, Jupiter tried to turn away from the wind, but Mr. Huff urged him back the way they had come. Reluctantly Jupiter plodded into the raging wind, carrying Mr. Huff toward home.

Mr. Huff looked back once and called to Pansy to follow, but he could no longer see the old mare. There was nothing he could do to help Pansy now.

Maybe it's just as well, he thought. If Pansy freezes to death, it will be the end of the matter with Janis.

Janis.

A yearning to see his daughter again so overwhelmed Mr. Huff that he nearly lost his balance and slid to the ground.

"I've seen enough," Warren said as he and Betsy staggered through another waist-high drift. He had to shout to be heard, even though Betsy was right beside him.

"What time is it?" Betsy yelled.

Warren pushed the small knob that made the dial of his watch light up. "Back home, it's two o'clock."

"We've only been here ten minutes."

"I don't care if it's ten seconds. I've never been so cold."

"Neither have I," Betsy admitted.

"It doesn't look any different now than it did when we got here. We could stay another hour and not learn anything new."

"Let's go home," Betsy said.

Warren unzipped his jacket and reached for the map, congratulating himself for having the foresight to put clear tape on it, to keep it dry. Without the map, he and Betsy would have no way to get home.

Warren's hands felt clumsy. Even with gloves on, his fingers were stiff from the cold, and he had a hard time getting the map out of his pocket.

As he handed the map to Betsy, a gust of wind snatched it out of his grasp.

Warren leaped in the air, grabbing for the map, but it swirled above his head, just out of his reach.

With her eyes on the map, Betsy crouched, ready to jump toward it if it came close to her.

The map circled twice above Warren's head and then swooped downward, in front of Betsy. She belly-flopped onto it, making sure it did not fly up again.

Pressing the map against her jacket with one arm, she stood up. "That was close," she said. Her knees shook.

"I'm sorry," Warren said. "My fingers are so stiff, I couldn't hold on to it."

Betsy nodded. She knew it wasn't Warren's fault. Her hands were stiff with cold, too.

Warren stood behind her and put his arms around her, feeling the Instant Commuter against his chest. He pressed on Betsy's arm, making sure the map didn't blow away again.

Betsy clamped her left hand tightly on his arm, and with her right hand, she touched the tip of the probe to the map.

Then she shoved the probe into her pocket, and held onto Warren's arm with both hands.

Warren closed his eyes and waited. He knew they wouldn't notice the wind on this trip, not with the wind already blowing like crazy.

Snow swirled around them; the air remained bitter cold.

They waited.

And waited.

We should be home by now, Warren thought. What's taking so long?

Betsy called over her shoulder, "Is the machine still running? I don't feel any vibration."

Warren opened his eyes.

"You didn't turn it off when we got here, did you?" he asked.

"No. I left it running."

"Hang on to the map," he said. "I'll check to see if the switch got turned off accidentally."

He tried to lift the flap on Betsy's backpack.

"I can't get the backpack open," Warren said. "It's frozen shut. The wind blew snow under the flap."

He used both hands to try to pry up the flap, but the backpack was a solid chunk of ice.

"We'd be home by now, if the Instant Commuter was working," Betsy said, fighting to keep the panic out of her voice.

"When it gets this cold, the whole machine

must freeze up whether it's turned on or not."

"Maybe we can use the matches to thaw it out," Betsy said.

Warren shoved his hand in his pocket and found the small box of matches. He struck a match; the wind instantly blew it out.

"Bend over," he said. "I'll lean over the backpack and shield the flame from the wind."

Betsy bent forward until her face was next to the top of the snowdrift. Warren stood beside her with his back to the wind.

"Don't set my coat on fire," Betsy said.

Warren held his hand as close to the top of the backpack as he could. He lit another match and held it next to the corner where he knew the On/Off switch was. The match burned down until Warren had to drop it in the snow to keep from scorching his fingers.

Nothing happened.

"This isn't going to work," he said.

"We'll have to keep walking," Betsy said, "until we find shelter, some place warm where we can thaw out the Instant Commuter."

But where, they both wondered, will that be? And will we find it in time?

CHAPTER

11

Janis could go no farther.

Her legs were stiff as tree trunks, and when she fell into yet another snowbank, she did not have enough strength left to stand up. It seemed as if her blood had turned to ice water, chilling her from the inside out.

Janis lay still, knowing that if she did not move, she would never move again. It didn't matter. All she wanted was to sink into sleep and have this terrible, freezing ordeal be over.

Slowly Janis closed her eyes and gave herself up to the cold.

Mr. Huff leaned forward against Jupiter's neck, trying to keep the horse warm, and trying to keep his own face out of the wind as much as possible.

The wagon, he knew, had not gone far before it got stuck. Less than half a mile, he guessed.

He had fed the horses before he hitched them, so if Jupiter could find his way, the horse should have enough stamina to make it home.

Mr. Huff could not tell whether Jupiter was still on the road. But they were going into the wind, and that was the right direction.

Jupiter stopped so abruptly that Mr. Huff nearly slid straight over the horse's shoulder. Mr. Huff dismounted and walked to Jupiter's head. Only then did he realize that they were standing beside the barn.

He had expected to see the barn light. The electric lines must be down.

Relief flooded through Mr. Huff as he opened the barn and went inside with Jupiter. He removed the blanket and rubbed down the horse as well as he could, given the condition of his own hands. Then he put the blanket back on Jupiter.

The temperature in the barn felt below freezing. But at least Jupiter was out of the wind.

Mr. Huff left the barn, hoping he could get to the house before he collapsed from exhaustion. He struggled forward, head down, forcing his tired body to move.

When he thought he had gone far enough, he stopped. Had he missed the house? Looking to his right, he saw a faint glimmer of light. He turned toward the light, realizing he had veered off course. If his wife had not left the oil lamp in the window, he would have gone past the house without seeing it.

He staggered inside and found his wife crying beside the stove.

"Janis didn't come?"

She shook her head, unable to tell him the terrible news.

"I couldn't make it to the Wilsons' place," he said. "I had to leave the wagon and abandon Pansy. I rode Jupiter, and he managed to find his way to the barn."

Mrs. Huff sobbed harder.

"We mustn't give up hope," he said as he took off his snow-covered coat. "Janis may be at the school still, or at home with one of her classmates."

Finally Mrs. Huff choked out the words. "Ellie's gone, too."

Mr. Huff stood as still as a snowman while she told him what had happened.

When she finished, he walked to the corner of the kitchen and picked up an old cornhusk doll. Mr. Huff hunched over, clutching the doll in his hands, and began to cry.

Seconds after Janis closed her eyes, something nudged against her cheek. She turned her head slightly, wanting only to be left alone. The nudge came again, more insistent.

Janis forced one hand toward her head, to push away whatever was bothering her. Her hand touched something that moved.

Janis struggled to open her eyes. A large dark shape loomed over her, inches from her face. The shock brought Janis back to full consciousness. She stared upward until the shape bent to nudge her again, and then she recognized who it was.

"Pansy," she whispered.

Pansy whinnied and shook her head, sprinkling Janis with clumps of snow.

Janis pushed herself into a sitting position.

Pansy pawed at the ground.

Hope put new strength in Janis's legs, and she struggled to her feet. She put her arms around Pansy's neck and tried to jump high enough to mount Pansy, but her legs were too weak. Her feet barely left the ground.

Instead of riding, Janis held fast to the tether, and when Pansy moved forward into the wind, Janis stumbled along beside her. She made no attempt to lead the horse; she did not even try to look where they were going. She simply clung to the tether and let Pansy guide her.

By staying close to Pansy, but slightly behind her front shoulder, Janis let the horse open a path through the thick drifts. Janis's weary legs no longer had to raise quite so high.

Pansy forged the way slowly, seeming to sense that Janis could not run. Or perhaps, Janis thought, Pansy is also too weary to move quickly in such conditions.

I saved Pansy's life on Saturday, Janis thought, when I stood between her and Daddy's shotgun. Perhaps today Pansy will save mine.

Betsy pushed her hands in front of herself, to shove her way through another snowbank. This time she felt something solid beneath the snow.

"Warren! This isn't just a snowbank. There's something here."

Both kids dug quickly, scraping the snow

away from the side of a tall mound. There was a hard surface under the snow.

Warren made a fist and whacked it down. His hand broke through a layer of ice.

Warren wiggled his fingers downward into the mound, trying to determine what it was.

"It's a haystack," Warren said. "Maybe we can tunnel into it and wait out the storm."

Beneath the snow, the entire haystack was coated with ice. They kicked at the bottom of the haystack, breaking loose chunks of ice. They pushed the chunks away and then chipped handfuls of hay free and pulled them away, slowly creating an opening into the middle of the haystack.

It was hard work. Because of the high wind, freezing rain had penetrated the haystack and now it was frozen nearly to the center. After digging for ten minutes, Betsy and Warren had only made an opening two feet deep.

"This isn't going to work," Betsy said. "We'll be exhausted before we can make a space big enough for both of us to get into."

"Let's set fire to the hay," Warren suggested. "Maybe we can thaw out the Instant Commuter."

"Great idea. If nothing else, a fire will help keep us warm."

The hay they had dug out had already blown away. They each pulled out another handful. This time, instead of tossing the hay behind them, they put it together in a small pile and Warren held it down while Betsy crouched over it and struck a match.

The match sputtered and went out.

"The hay is frozen," she said.

"Keep trying in the same place," Warren said. "Maybe we can dry it out enough for it to catch on fire."

Betsy lit another match. And another. And another.

On the sixth try the hay flared up. Warren cupped his hands around the flame, to shield it from the wind. Betsy lit another match and held it close to the hay that was burning. That area caught fire, too.

Smoke rose from the pieces of hay next to the flaming one. Betsy lit more matches.

Soon all of the small pile of hay was either burning or smoking, but the wind blew most of the heat away. Even when they stood directly beside the fire, choking on the smoke, it was not hot enough to penetrate their clothing.

While Betsy tried to shield the fire from the wind, Warren dug out more hay and added it to the fire, taking care not to quench the flame. He added more and more hay until the fire was a foot square.

The bigger their fire got, the more quickly the hay caught when Warren put it in.

"You feed the fire," Warren said. "I'll hold the Instant Commuter next to the heat."

He helped Betsy unbuckle the backpack and take it off.

Betsy yanked more hay from inside the stack and threw it on the fire.

Warren held the backpack as close to the flames as he could, turning it frequently so that all sides got warm. The ice melted and dripped into the fire. Warren pried the backpack open and held the flap up, exposing the Instant Commuter switch. He held that part toward the fire.

"Don't drop it," Betsy said.

Warren clutched the machine as tightly as he could, wishing she had not said that. He held the probe against the side of the Instant Commuter so that it got warm at the same time.

The flames climbed higher and got hotter. Although the wind made the flames dip and bow, the fire was strong enough to continue burning.

By staying downwind, Betsy and Warren felt the heat. Their eyes watered from the smoke, but it didn't matter. The warmth was so welcome, they didn't care how much smoke blew in their faces.

As Betsy flung fists full of hay into the fire, Warren began to get some feeling back in his fingers.

"I can feel my hands again," he said. "If they're getting warm, the Instant Commuter is, too. I think this will work."

He continued to rotate the Instant Commuter until Betsy stopped throwing hay on the fire and stood with her hands extended over the flames.

"Ice melts under pressure," Betsy said. "That's what makes ice skating possible."

Warren coughed as ashes rose into his face.

"Ice melts under the skates and forms a film of water on which the skater slides," Betsy said. "If it's so cold that the weight of the skater isn't enough to melt the ice, skating is impossible."

"Then nobody's skating around here," Warren said. "I don't know how cold it is, but it feels like fifty below zero."

"Maybe we should press our hands hard

against the Instant Commuter and see if that helps," Betsy said.

"I think the machine is as warm as it's going to get," Warren said. "Let's try it again."

He jiggled the On/Off switch, and a thin piece of ice dropped into the fire. Warren felt the machine vibrate.

"It's on!" he yelled. "Quick! Let's get out of here while we can."

Betsy pulled the map from her pocket while Warren slipped the backpack on over his coat. He didn't bother to buckle the strap. He grabbed Betsy, to be sure they stayed together.

As Warren thrust the tip of the probe toward the map, Betsy yelled, "Stop!"

Warren jerked his hand back.

"What's the matter?" he asked.

"What was that?" Betsy said.

"What was what?"

"Listen," Betsy said.

Warren listened.

A small voice, so faint he wasn't sure he had heard it, floated toward them on the wind.

"Help!" the voice cried. "Daddy! Help me!"

CHAPTER

12

Warren and Betsy stared at each other, both thinking the same thing.

"If we go to see who it is," Warren said, "the Instant Commuter will probably freeze up again."

"We could lose our chance to go home," Betsy said.

"We might freeze to death."

The voice came again. "Help! Daddy! I'm lost!"

"It sounds like a little kid," Betsy said.

"He must be close or we'd never hear him," Warren said.

"We can't leave a little kid out here alone."

"Let's build up the fire, so it doesn't go out

while we look for him." They grabbed more hay and put it on the fire.

When the flames were a foot high, Betsy said, "Let's go. If we are only gone a couple of minutes, the fire won't go out."

Warren faced the direction he thought the voice had come from and yelled, "Hello! Where are you?"

"Here!" cried the voice.

Betsy and Warren turned away from the fire and into the raging wind.

Betsy led the way toward the sound with Warren right behind her. They had gone only a few yards when Betsy felt as if she had unexpectedly stepped off a curb. When her foot went forward, the ground was not where she expected it to be.

"Oh!" she said as she skidded downward on her heel, trying to keep her balance.

When she stopped, her head was even with Warren's knees. "I stepped in a hole," she said.

"Don't move," he said. "I'll pull you out."

Warren slid his feet slowly through the snow, feeling for the hole. He didn't want to drop into a well or a gravel pit.

"I think it's a ditch," Betsy said. "It goes

up on either side of me, but I can walk straight ahead."

"Help!" the voice called. It was closer now, ahead of Betsy in the ditch.

"If I lean over, I'm sheltered from the wind down here," Betsy said.

Warren skidded down into the ditch beside her. The ditch did offer some protection from the wind; it was a welcome relief not to have the snow constantly blowing in his face.

Warren and Betsy followed the ditch, hurrying as fast as they could toward the person who needed help.

"Keep talking!" Betsy shouted. "We can't see you!"

"Mommy?" Ellie said. "Here I am! In the snow!"

"We're coming!" Warren hollered.

They expected to find the child standing in the snow. Betsy nearly tripped over her before she saw her, lying in the ditch.

Betsy stopped abruptly and clutched Warren's sleeve. "Down there," she said.

Warren and Betsy crouched beside the frightened child.

"We're here," Warren said. "You'll be okay now."

But will we? he wondered. Have we traded our own lives for a chance to save hers?

Janis stumbled along beside Pansy.

The horse walked with her head down, keeping her nose close to the ground as the top of her head broke a path through the drifts. The wind whipped her mane and lifted the corners of the blanket that Mr. Huff had snugged around her middle. Snow froze around her hooves, making them heavy. Pansy plodded on.

Janis kept her head bent, not knowing or caring where she was. She felt like a windup toy instead of a real girl. Her body kept going with no thought from Janis, and it would keep on going until it wound down. Janis did not look up until Pansy stopped.

Then Janis raised her eyes slowly, almost too tired to wonder why Pansy wasn't moving.

Pansy whinnied and pawed her front hoof on the ground beside the barn door.

Slowly the realization sank into Janis's brain.

"We're home," Janis said. "You did it, Pansy! We're home!" She lifted the wooden latch and held the barn door open for Pansy.

The horse walked straight to her stall and waited beside it.

Janis felt for the light switch, but when she pushed it, nothing happened. The electric lines must be down.

Feeling her way, Janis staggered forward and put Pansy in the stall, but she did not have enough strength left to climb into the loft and throw hay down. Instead, she poured a cup of grain into Pansy's feed trough. That would have to do for now.

She was tempted to stay in the barn. She heard Jupiter moving about in the next stall. Farther back in the darkness, she could hear the cattle shifting position, too.

Although it was bitter cold in the barn, she was at least out of the wind, and the body heat from the animals should be enough to keep her from freezing. Maybe she ought to stay in the stall with Pansy, rather than trying to make it to the house.

But Mother and Daddy would have a fire in the stove—a warm, blazing fire that would penetrate her bones. Janis felt her way to the tack room, where Daddy stored seed.

She emptied a gunnysack containing corn seed and used the tine of a pitchfork to poke two holes in the gunnysack. She pulled the sack over her head, adjusting it so she could see out the holes.

Her ears hurt when the burlap sack touched them. Janis knew her ears were badly frostbitten. She had heard about a man in Vergas who had no fingers because they were frozen when he was a boy. Gangrene had set in, and his fingers had fallen off.

Janis wished she had been able to wear a gunnysack earlier. What if her ears fell off?

With the gunnysack on her head, she opened the barn door and started in the direction of the house.

Half an hour earlier, before Pansy nudged her awake, Janis did not think she could take one more step. But now, when she was nearly there, sheer willpower kept her legs moving.

Her brief time in the barn, out of the wind, had helped, too. Thinking about the warm fire that awaited her, Janis pushed on. Bump! She ran into something hard. Her heart raced, hoping it was the side of the house, but when she stuck her hands out and felt the structure, she knew it was only the chicken shed.

I'm too far to the right, Janis realized, and she changed her course. Ahead, she saw a small faint glow of light. A light in the window? Keep going, she told herself, knowing she was almost home. Don't give up now.

She followed the light until she saw the dark outline of the house. Stretching her arms in front of her, she lunged the last few feet to the kitchen door. Her hands were too frozen to turn the doorknob, so she pounded on the door with her palms.

Mr. Huff opened the door, and Janis fell forward into his arms. She was too weak, and too cold, to speak.

Mr. Huff pulled the gunnysack from Janis's head, but her clothes were frozen to her body. Mrs. Huff had to use a butcher knife to cut Janis's sweater and dress off her.

Mrs. Huff wrapped Janis in a blanket while Mr. Huff put her feet in the dishpan and poured cold water on her shoes to loosen the ice so that he could get her shoes and socks off.

"She's too frozen to use hot water," he said. "The pain would be terrible."

"Start with cold water, and gradually add warm," Mrs. Huff said. "Oh, Janis, we were so worried. Oh, my poor darling."

Janis's teeth chattered. Even wrapped in a blanket and sitting beside the stove, she couldn't stop shaking. As the feeling returned to her hands and feet, they ached more than they had outside. Before, they were numb; now she could feel the pain.

No one spoke it out loud, but Mr. and Mrs. Huff and Janis all had the same worry: Would Janis lose her feet? Possibly even her legs? What about her hands, and her ears? Many times amputation was the only option for patients with severe frostbite.

When Janis finally quit shivering enough to talk, she told them how Pansy had awakened her and led her home.

"Pansy saved my life," Janis said.

Mr. Huff, who was holding one of Janis's hands between his own to warm it, paused and said, "Yes, she did. She surely did. And if Pansy lives through this night, I will spare her life."

For the first time since Doc Swenson's visit, Janis smiled.

"Pansy deserves to live out her days with us," Mr. Huff said, "whether she can work or not."

"Thank you, Daddy."

"But the cold and the effort of walking through the snow may take its toll on such an old horse," Mr. Huff warned. "Pansy may not survive the strain. Or her legs may be too badly frozen."

Mrs. Huff patted Janis's shoulder. "I hope she lives," Mrs. Huff said.

Janis realized that there had been no questions about her ordeal from her sister, which was most unusual. She glanced around the kitchen.

"Where's Ellie?" she asked.

She saw identical looks of sorrow and horror flash across the faces of her parents, and she knew, even before they told her, that Ellie was missing.

CHAPTER

13

When Ellie heard voices shout that they were coming to get her, she assumed it was Mommy and Daddy. No one else would be looking for her, because no one else knew she was lost. Not even Janis and Wonderful.

"Hurry!" she screamed.

Before she could yell again, a boy and a girl appeared beside her. They pulled her to her feet.

Crying with relief, Ellie threw her arms around the girl and held on.

"Where do you live?" Warren asked. "Are we near your house?"

"I don't know," Ellie said. "I got lost."

"A ditch like this would most likely go along the side of a road," Betsy said. "Let's walk in it, and see where it leads."

"I can't walk any more," Ellie said. "My feet won't work."

"We'll all freeze if we don't keep moving," Warren said.

"You could carry me," Ellie said.

"You're too big," Betsy said.

"I'm four. My name is Ellie."

"Maybe I can carry her back to the haystack," Warren said. "We'll build up the fire again. If she gets warmer, she may be able to walk."

He picked up Ellie, turned around, and trudged back in the direction they had just come. The child was heavy, and he was already worn out. He was not sure he could make it all the way back to the haystack.

He felt her shivering as he held her against his chest, and was glad they had not ignored her cry for help.

"Don't worry, Ellie," he said. "We made a fire, and you can sit right next to it."

"Are you friends of Janis?"

"Who's Janis?"

While Ellie told him about Janis, and about Wonderful, Warren kept looking over the top of the ditch, hoping to see the glow of their small fire.

"I don't see anything, but I smell smoke," Betsy said. "Let's climb out of the ditch here."

"You'll have to climb up by yourself," Warren told Ellie. "I can't carry you up the slope."

He put her on her feet and left her standing there while he scrambled up the side of the ditch. Betsy climbed up beside him. They leaned down, and each grasped one of Ellie's hands. Pulling together, they lifted her out of the ditch.

Ellie began to cry. "I don't like the wind," she sobbed. "It's too cold and the snow gets in my eyes."

Warren again scooped the little girl into his arms, and she buried her face in his shoulder while he struggled through the drifting snow.

Betsy went ahead of them, trying to shield the child and clear a path for Warren.

"I see a tiny light!" Betsy cried. "It must be what's left of our fire."

By the time they got to the haystack, the light was out, and the blackened circle where the hay had burned was already covered over with a faint sifting of new snow.

Warren put Ellie down. He and Betsy quickly pulled more hay from the stack. They put it in the same spot, knowing the ground there would be warmer and drier than anywhere else.

This time it took four matches for the hay to catch, but soon they had made a big enough fire that they could feel heat rising toward their outstretched hands.

They fed the fire more slowly then, wanting to make the hay last as long as possible.

"Where is your house?" Ellie said. "I never saw you before."

"We don't live in Minnesota," Betsy said. "We live in Washington State. We're just visiting."

"How did you get here?" Ellie asked. "Who brought you?"

"We flew," Betsy said, "but not in an airplane."

"You flew by yourselves?" Ellie said.

"Yes," Warren said, "and we need to go home soon, or we'll be missed."

Betsy knew what Warren was telling her, and he was right. He and Betsy had expected to be away from Warren's house for half an hour or less, and she guessed it was already close to two hours.

The Blizzard Disaster

Her parents and Warren's grandma did not have any idea where they were. It was time to walk Mongo again, and if Betsy didn't come home soon, Mom would telephone Warren's grandma.

"If we don't go home while we have the fire to keep the Instant Commuter thawed out," Warren said, "we may not be able to go back at all. Ever." He looked at Ellie and added, "But how can we leave a four-year-old alone in the worst blizzard of the century?"

"We can't," Betsy said. "We have to stay with her."

"All three of us might freeze," Warren said.

"Jump up and down," Betsy said. "We need to keep our blood circulating."

They jumped a few times, then stopped. They were too tired. And even with the fire, their feet and legs were as cold and heavy as concrete.

"Let's take her home with us," Betsy said.

"Three of us, on one Instant Commuter?"

"It might work. She doesn't weigh much."

"You didn't carry her through the snow," Warren said. "What would we do after we got her home? We can't hide a four-year-old in the closet."

Peg Kehret

"We'd have to tell the truth," Betsy said. "Mom and Dad would understand."

"So would my mom," Warren said, "and Gram. But the Instant Commuter would not be a secret any longer. And what about her family? She'd never see them again."

"They would think she was lost and frozen in the storm," Betsy said. "They probably think that already. And if we don't get her out of here soon, it will be true. For her, and for us."

Warren removed his backpack and held the Instant Commuter close to the flames. He held the probe close to the fire, too, making sure every part of the machine was as warm as possible.

The wind swept snow up from the ground and puffed it across the fire, nearly extinguishing the flames. Warren hunched over the Instant Commuter, to protect it while Betsy put more hay on the fire. He kept trying to think of another solution to their problem, something that would save Ellie's life without separating her from her family.

Long ago Warren had asked Grandpa how he could think of so many inventions. Grandpa had said, "I always try to come up with more than one way to solve a problem.

114

Sometimes my first idea is the best one, but often it isn't. So I never stop with just one possibility; I always try to think of alternatives."

What alternative was there in this situation? *Think!* Warren told himself as he rotated the Instant Commuter over the fire.

"I have an idea," Warren said, "that would get Ellie back with her family. After we take her with us to Gram's house, we'll bring her back, but instead of using the picture of the storm, we'll use one of those other photos that were taken a day or two after the storm was over."

"Yes!" Betsy said. "We'll take her to the University of Minnesota football stadium. She'll be found there right away, and returned to her parents."

"That should create some excitement," Warren said. "They'll never believe her when she tells them how she got there."

"It doesn't matter," Betsy said. "She'll be alive."

"I don't want to go to a football game," Ellie said. "I want to go home."

"You're going to go home," Warren said. "I hope."

"Let's try it," Betsy said.

Warren turned on the Instant Commuter.

"It's working," he said. "I feel the vibration." Quickly he slipped the backpack on and buckled the strap.

"Ellie," Betsy said, "we're going to take you on a trip to Washington. Won't that be fun?"

"No," said Ellie. "I don't want to go to Washington. I want to go see Janis and Wonderful."

Betsy took the map of home out of her coat pocket.

"Hold on to me, Ellie," Betsy said, "as tightly as you can." She took the little girl's hand and pulled her close. Then, with Ellie between them, she put her arms around Warren.

Warren touched the map with the tip of the probe.

The Instant Commuter, which was designed to run silently, made a grinding sound.

"What's that?" Ellie asked. She tried to move out of Betsy's grasp, to look behind Warren.

"Hold still!" Betsy said.

Snow pelted the three children on their backs. They stayed where they were.

Warren listened to the grinding sound for

116

ten seconds, and then turned the Instant Commuter off. "It's too much weight," he said. "I'm afraid we'll wreck it if we keep trying."

"We'll have to travel separately," Betsy said. "One of us will take Ellie to your house, and then use the other photo to take her to the football stadium. Leave Ellie there, and come back here, and we'll go home together."

"What's a photo?" Ellie asked. "What are you talking about?"

Warren shook his head. "The one who travels would never find this exact spot again. Our only target is that blurry picture of the blizzard. One of us would be stuck here by the haystack, and the other one would be wandering around in the storm."

"We can't leave her, and we can't take her with us," Betsy said. "We'll have to stay."

"Great," Warren said. "Instead of just one kid freezing to death, all three of us will."

"I want to go home," Ellie said.

"So do we," said Betsy. "So do we."

CHAPTER
14

"Maybe the storm will stop soon," Betsy said. "Maybe someone will rescue us."

"And maybe not," Warren said.

"Are you saying you want to go home and leave her here by herself?" Betsy asked.

Warren thought a moment. "No," he said. "We have to stay."

"I'm hungry," Ellie said. "I didn't have any supper."

"I'm hungry, too," Warren said. He pulled more hay from the haystack and spread it on the fire.

"I want bread and gravy," Ellie said, "and some raspberry sauce from the cellar."

"Not me," Warren said. "I'll have a large pizza with extra cheese, and a double order of fries."

"And some hot chocolate," Betsy said.

"What's pizza?" Ellie asked.

Warren and Ellie exchanged surprised glances. In their struggle to get through the blizzard, they had forgotten that they had traveled nearly sixty years into the past.

"Pizza is a kind of pie," Warren said. "There's a crust that's covered with tomato sauce and cheese and lots of toppings."

"That's a funny kind of pie," Ellie said. "My mommy makes apple pie. Wonderful likes apple pie."

The wind shifted suddenly. Smoke swirled in their faces, and they moved to the other side of the fire.

"Years ago in East Africa," said Betsy, "people made white ant pie."

"You're making this up," Warren said. "Aren't you?"

"It's true. They mixed white ants with banana flour and it made a sweet candy called white ant pie."

"I'd rather have apple pie," Ellie said. "Or bread pudding."

"I can not believe," Warren said, "that we

are standing in a blizzard in the year 1940, in serious danger of never going home again, while you give us the recipe for white ant pie. Where do you get this stuff? Don't you ever read any normal books?"

"Maybe Daddy will see our fire," Ellie said. "When he comes to look for me, he might see it, because the haystack is right across the road from our house."

"You mean, we're close to where you live?" Warren said.

"I live across the road. I can see the haystack from the window in Janis's room."

"Which way?" Betsy asked. "Do you know which way your house is?"

Ellie shook her head. "I tried to go home, but I couldn't see and I got all mixed up and then I got stuck in the snow."

"But you're sure this haystack can be seen from your house? Maybe there's more than one haystack."

"No," said Ellie. "There's only one. Daddy put the rest of the hay in the barn for Jupiter and Pansy."

"Let's burn the whole haystack," Warren said. "Maybe it will give off enough light that we'll be able to find the house."

Betsy and Warren piled fresh hay on the fire as fast as they could. The hay was dryer, now that they were farther into the middle of the haystack, and it blazed up quickly.

"We could throw some burning hay into the middle of the haystack," Betsy suggested, "and try to start a fire from the inside out."

"Good idea. Let's do it." Warren kicked part of the burning hay into the area they had scooped out.

Betsy did the same.

Using the sides of their boots, they shoved the flaming hay inside the haystack. Thick smoke poured out the opening, making it impossible to see what they were doing.

"We should have made a chimney," Warren said. He went part way around the haystack, brushed snow off an area level with his shoulders, and pounded on the cleared area until the layer of ice crumbled. Then he pulled hay from that section, trying to let more oxygen into the center of the haystack and give the smoke a place to get out.

Betsy knelt beside the original opening, with her head turned away from the smoke. She pulled tufts of hay from the edges and threw them far enough inside so that they touched the fire and ignited.

She continued to feed the fire that way until so much smoke poured from the opening that she was forced to move away.

Warren tugged hay away from the other side. After he removed several fistfuls, smoke followed the hay out the hole. The smoke was quickly followed by bright red and yellow flames, shooting up from the "chimney" Warren had crafted.

The snow and ice on the top of the haystack began to melt. As the hay thawed, water dripped down into the fire, hissing like an angry cat.

Warren hurried around the haystack and stood beside Betsy and Ellie. When they faced the fire, it felt warm on their faces. They held their hands toward it and stood as close as they could, with the wind at their backs so the smoke didn't get in their eyes.

"My front feels like toast," Betsy said, "and my back like an icicle."

All at once the whole top of the haystack burst into flame. The snow on the ground around them glowed orange. New snowflakes fell into the bright circle of light and turned to steam.

"Let's walk away from the haystack while

it's bright like this," Warren said. "We'll go as far as we can without losing sight of the fire. Maybe we'll be able to see Ellie's house."

They set off together, with Ellie in the middle. Smoke, chased by the wind, followed them.

"Look for lights," Betsy said. "They'll have a porch light on, and lights in the windows."

They saw only darkness, and endless snow.

They kept going until the fire was merely an orange glow behind them. Then they turned left, and went that direction, making sure they always kept the glow of the fire within sight.

They saw no buildings in the distance, and Ellie didn't recognize any landmark that gave a clue to which direction her house was.

When they had circled the burning haystack without success, they returned to warm themselves. The flames were lower now and the heat was less intense.

"The fire is starting to die down," Betsy said.

"How will we stay warm if the fire goes out?" Ellie asked.

Betsy and Warren looked at each other, but neither of them had an answer.

*   *   *

Mr. and Mrs. Huff carried blankets downstairs and made a bed for Janis on the floor beside the stove. With one blanket underneath her and the rest piled on top of her, she fell asleep instantly.

Her parents agreed to take turns watching out the window for any sign of Ellie. One would watch, while the other one rested beside Janis.

However, neither of them wanted to rest first, and they finally admitted they could not relax long enough to sleep. Instead they stood together by the window, holding the oil lamp and staring out into the snow.

Periodically they opened the door and shouted Ellie's name into the wind. And every few minutes Mr. Huff would hurry into the cold living room and call out that door, as well.

On one of Mr. Huff's trips to the living room, Mrs. Huff looked toward the road again, and then set the lamp on the window ledge. She cupped her hands on the sides of her eyes and pressed her face against the window.

"Luke!" she shouted. "Come here!"

As he rushed to join her, she said, "Look!

See that light? I think there's a fire across the road."

They stared for a moment at the odd orange glow. "It must be the haystack," Mr. Huff said. "That's the direction it is, and there's nothing else in the field that would burn."

"Who would set fire to our haystack?"

"Maybe it got hit by lightning," Mr. Huff said.

"I haven't seen any lightning," Mrs. Huff said, "or heard any thunder."

"Perhaps someone started a fire on purpose," Mr. Huff said, "to keep from freezing."

Mrs. Huff put her hand on his arm. "Do you think," she whispered, "that Ellie could somehow have started a fire?"

"I don't know. I'm going over there."

"I'm going with you."

They jerked their boots on and dressed once more in their heavy coats, hats, and gloves.

"We'll need to use the clothesline," Mrs. Huff said. "We'll walk straight enough toward the fire, with the light to guide us, but coming home we'll have the light at our backs."

Mr. Huff made sure the clothesline was securely tied to the doorknob.

Side by side, they stepped out the door into the wind and hurried toward the orange glow. It was dimmer now than it had been when they first saw it, but Mr. Huff knew exactly where his haystack was, and he headed toward it.

Betsy said, "If the Instant Commuter won't carry all three of us, we'll have to go separately. You take Ellie home, and then take her to the stadium. I'll stay here."

"I won't leave you."

"You can come back for me."

Warren shook his head.

The fire flickered in the wind. They knew it would not last much longer.

"If we all stay," Betsy said, "we are all going to freeze. If you go, you'll save Ellie for sure, and maybe you *will* be able to find me when you come back."

"You go," Warren said. "I'll stay here and wait for you to come back and find me."

They faced each other grimly.

"We'll draw straws," Betsy said.

Warren agreed. He took a long piece of hay that had blown off the fire, and broke off two pieces. One was four inches long, the other was only two inches. He explained to Ellie how to hold the pieces of hay so that one end of each was even and the other end didn't show.

Ellie clutched the hay in her fists.

Betsy drew first. She got the short piece.

CHAPTER

15

"I'll find you again," Warren promised. "I'll put the probe on different parts of the blizzard photo until I find you. I'll come back a hundred times, if I have to."

"Hold on to Warren, Ellie," Betsy said. "He's going to take you to a warm house in Washington State, and then to a football stadium where some other people will find you and take you home."

"I don't want to go to a football game," Ellie said. "I want to go home right now." She began to cry.

Betsy tried to calm Ellie and explain to her where Warren was taking her.

The tired child was past being reasonable.

Even when Betsy and Warren assured her that she would be back home with her parents soon, Ellie continued to cry.

"Just take her," Betsy said, "before the machine freezes up again."

Warren turned the switch to on. The Instant Commuter vibrated into action.

"It's running," Warren said.

Betsy took Ellie's hand and pulled her close to Warren so that he could hold on to her.

"No!" Ellie said. "You go to Washington with Warren. I want to stay here." She yanked her hand away and ran to the other side of the fire.

"Ellie, come back here," Betsy said. She followed Ellie around the smoldering remains of the fire; Warren went around the other way.

In those few seconds between words, they heard a man's voice behind them. "Hello!" he shouted. "We see your fire!"

"It's Daddy!" Ellie said, her tears forgotten.

"We're coming!" a woman shouted.

"And Mommy!"

Ellie dashed away from the fire, and away from Betsy and Warren, toward the voices. "Here I am!" she screamed.

"Ellie!" Two adult voices responded at the same time.

"Ellie! Keep calling!"

The fire flickered dimly.

Warren ran to stand beside Betsy. "Let's go," he said.

Betsy gripped Warren's coat while Warren touched the probe to the map that showed Gram's street.

As they waited for the Instant Commuter to work, the wind gusted, carrying happy voices toward them.

"Ellie! It's really you!"

"Mommy! Daddy! I want to go home."

"Oh, Ellie, we've been so worried."

Warren and Betsy smiled. The strong wind grew warmer, and they knew they were leaving the blizzard behind.

The wind stopped. Betsy and Warren looked around and saw that they were near Gram's house. They went inside and climbed the stairs to Warren's room, where their trip had begun. Warren removed the backpack and put the Instant Commuter on the table.

They took off their coats, then sank wearily onto the chairs.

"My coat and hat are perfectly dry," Betsy said. "There's no ice on my boots. It's as if we experienced the blizzard in virtual reality, instead of actually being there."

"We were there, all right," Warren said. "I've never been so cold, or so tired."

"When we're in a different time," Betsy said, "we are there completely. But when we get home, it's as if we never left."

"I wonder what would have happened to Ellie," Warren said, "if we had not found her."

"She might have died."

"Do you really believe we went back in time and changed the outcome of an event that took place all those years ago?"

"I want to think we did." Betsy smiled. "Little Ellie is more than sixty years old now."

Warren looked at the clock beside his bed. It said 4:15.

"We survived a blizzard and maybe saved a little girl's life," he said, "and we were only gone two hours and fifteen minutes."

"It felt like two weeks," Betsy replied. "I'm going home to walk Mongo. And then I plan to take a long, hot shower."

Mrs. Huff carried Ellie to the house.

Janis sat up when the door opened. "You found her!" she said.

"Did your feet get cold, Janis?" Ellie said.

131

"Mine did. But then I stood by the fire, and I wasn't so cold anymore."

"How did you start a fire?" Mr. Huff asked after Ellie's wet clothes had been removed and she was wrapped in a blanket.

"Betsy and Warren started the fire."

"Who?" Mrs. Huff said. "Was someone out there with you?"

"They found me in the ditch," Ellie said, "and Warren carried me because I couldn't walk, and they made the fire."

"You should have told us you weren't alone," Mr. Huff said, reaching once more for his coat. "I'll go back for them."

"They aren't there now, Daddy," Ellie said. "They went home to Washington, where they live. They can fly in the air, all by themselves, and when they get home they're going to eat pizza and white ant pie."

"Imaginary friends," Mrs. Huff said. "She's invented imaginary friends."

"Tell me the truth, Ellie," Mr. Huff said. "How did you start the fire?"

"I already told you," Ellie said. "Betsy and Warren made the fire."

"I have never," said Mrs. Huff, "known a child with such an imagination."

"I'm hungry," said Ellie.

The Blizzard Disaster

"I suppose it doesn't matter how the fire started," Mr. Huff said as he put soup in a cup for Ellie.

"Wonderful is hungry, too," said Ellie. "He wants ginger cookies."

The next morning, when Mr. Huff tried to open the living-room door, it was snowed shut. When he went out the kitchen door, he found drifts twenty and thirty feet high. The wind had packed the snow till it was hard as stone. Ellie put on her winter coat and walked across the drifts without sinking in.

She walked to the chestnut tree. "Look, Daddy," she called. "I can sit in the tree with Wonderful."

Mr. Huff walked across the drifts to the cornfield. When he returned, he said, "I found the rest of the cattle. They're frozen stiff. All we can do is skin them and use the hides."

"You saved what you could," Mrs. Huff said. "And we still have the chickens."

The day after their trip to the blizzard, Warren went to Betsy's house to meet Mongo. The gray-and-white shaggy dog bounced up and down like a yo-yo on the end of the leash.

"He *is* huge," Warren said.

"Sit, Mongo," Betsy said.

Mongo lunged toward Warren and slurped him on the hand.

"Old English sheepdogs," Betsy said, "should really be called New English sheepdogs. They've only been around a little over two hundred years, which isn't old when you're talking about dog breeds. Some breeds go back two or three thousand years."

"As soon as we exercise Mongo," Warren said, "let's write down everything we remember about the blizzard. I'd like to get our report finished early because I'm going out for track this year. I won't have as much free time once practice starts."

"Here's your chance to practice running," Betsy said, and she handed Warren the leash. Mongo trotted down the sidewalk, tugging as hard as he could to urge Warren to go faster.

"I have an idea for our report," Betsy said as she jogged beside Warren. "Let's pretend we are Ellie and write the report as a story. We can put in something about her sister and her imaginary squirrel, and then we can show Ellie getting lost in the blizzard."

"She could start a bonfire that gets noticed, and that's how she's rescued," Warren said.

"Mr. Munson loves it when a written report is creative. What could be more creative than a story?"

"What should we call it?" Warren asked.

"How about *The Blizzard Disaster?*"

"Perfect," said Warren.

It was three days before the Huffs' road was plowed and the telephone line repaired. Their first call was to Dr. Morgan, asking him to come and examine Janis.

"Did you lose a camera?" Dr. Morgan asked as he came in. "I found this on the side of the road. It must have been tossed up by the snowplow."

"It's Miss Colby's camera," Janis said. "She let me borrow it, but when I fell in the snow, I couldn't hold on to it."

"Miss Colby didn't make it home in the storm," Dr. Morgan said.

Janis held her breath, fearing his next words.

"She survived the blizzard," Dr. Morgan said, "by crawling in Fred Wilson's hog shed and staying all night with the hogs. When Fred started to dig out his hogs the next morning, he heard a voice call to him from inside. It gave him quite a start."

"I hope her camera isn't broken," Janis said.

"I clicked the shutter once," Dr. Morgan said. "It seems to be all right."

"Never mind the camera," Mrs. Huff said. "Is Janis all right?"

The doctor examined Janis and then said, "You may lose a toe or two, but that's all. You were lucky. Some of my patients didn't make it home, and one has already had a leg amputated just below the knee. The frostbite was so severe, it killed the tissue."

He examined Ellie next and proclaimed her perfectly fit, with no lasting problems from her ordeal.

As the doctor prepared to leave, Ellie said, "You have to examine Wonderful. He was lost in the storm, too."

"Is Wonderful the blind horse that Doc Swenson told me about?"

"It's Ellie's imaginary squirrel," Mrs. Huff explained.

"I'm sorry about your horse going blind. It's always hard to destroy an animal, especially one that's given you good service."

"We've decided to keep the blind horse," Mrs. Huff said. "She saved Janis's life."

"She guided me home," Janis said. "Without Pansy, I would not have made it."

"And the horse survived the ordeal?"

"A third of the flesh and bone on Pansy's tail fell off, due to being frozen," Mr. Huff said. "But that was the only ill effect she had from being out in the blizzard."

"Wonderful's tail froze off, too," said Ellie, "but he grew a new one."

To learn more about blizzards:

All Hell Broke Loose: The Story of How Young Minnesota People Coped with the November 11, 1940, Armistice Day Storm, the Worst Blizzard Ever to Hit Minnesota
  William H. Hull
  W H Hull (Edina, MN, 1985)

Blizzard
  Christopher Lampton
  The Millbrook Press (Brookfield, CT, 1991)

Blizzards
  Steven Otfinoski
  Twenty-first Century Books (New York, NY, 1994)

Blizzards and Winter Weather
  Dennis Brindell Frudin
  Children's Press (Chicago, IL, 1983)

In All Its Fury: The Story of the January 12, 1888, Blizzard
  W. H. O'Gara
  D. Jenkins (Lincoln, NE, 1975)